PEOPLE
AND LIFE'S SHOCKS

D. W. Herbert

GU00707449

ARTHUR H. STOCKWELL LTD
Torrs Park Ilfracombe Devon
Established 1898
www.ahstockwell.co.uk

British Library Cataloguing-in-Publication Data.
A catalogue record for this book is available
from the British Library.

This is an entirely fictional story,
and no conscious attempt has been made
to accurately record or recreate
any real-life events.

By the same author:
The RAF and the Chosen One

ISBN 978-0-7223-4102-5
Printed in Great Britain by
Arthur H. Stockwell Ltd
Torrs Park   Ilfracombe
Devon

CONTENTS

Smuggler's Retreat   5

Love, Fate and Marriage   47

SMUGGLER'S RETREAT

Dawn was just breaking as the drone of the last aircraft drifted from earshot. A deathly hush fell over London, as it always did while the people waited for the all-clear. Nobody moved until then. The people of the East End had learnt through bitter experience that there could always be a straggler or another wave of bombers coming in.

As the waiting went on, from No. 12 East Street, which was just between Commercial Road and the river, came a quiet sobbing. It was May – or, to be more precise, Mrs May Hawks. She lay under the big kitchen table in the scullery with her husband, Sam Hawks, and beside them slept their twelve-year-old daughter, Betty.

Sam mouthed, "Do leave off, girl. It's more than likely over now."

May came back like a flash: "I'll bloody well leave off when I wants," she snorted with a touch of anger in with her tears. She blew hard into her already wet hanky and went on, quieter now: "I'm not staying in this house any more in no raid. I'm going to the Tube like everybody else does – and, what's more, you're coming with me. If that daft old sod upstairs won't come, he can bloody well stay and get blown up."

"That's it – on and on! Blimey, I ain't never known a woman go on like you. Ain't I told you to go to the Tube, ain't I? You knows damn well I can't go and leave the old man up there on

5

his own – he's been good to you and me. So shut your big fat mouth before you wake the kid."

It was too late.

At this outburst, Betty stirred, looked at her mother and said in a sleepy voice, "'As it gone, Mum?"

"Not yet, love," sniffed May. "It might not be long. Try and rest, there's a good girl."

No more was said, and in five minutes the all-clear sounded. May crawled from under the table, telling Betty and Sam to get to bed and she would fetch them a drink. The gas wasn't on, and the water was off as well, but May had a small oil stove and she always filled two big pans with water each night so she was never without when it was cut off, which was nearly every time there was an air raid. That night's was one of the longest she had known.

'It must have gone on for five hours,' she thought as she lit the little oil stove.

While she was waiting for the water to boil she took down the blackout curtains and peered out into the early morning sunlight over the back garden. At first she could not quite make out what was wrong; then it dawned on her. At this time of day this side of the house should have been in the shadow of Mrs Steel's house in the next street. Her eyes lifted up to where it had been last night.

"My God, it's gone and so have nearly all the others and our garden wall," she murmured under her breath.

Just then Betty called from upstairs: "Mum, there's white stuff all over my bed. What shall I do?"

Before May had chance to answer, Sam called out, "OK, girl, I'll see to it." After a slight pause she heard Sam say, "Bugger me! Half the ceiling's down. Just you go and see if your granddad's all right while I shift this lot, Betsy."

Betty tripped along the landing in her bare feet, gently opened her granddad's door and peered in. There he was, flat on his back, mouth wide open, slightly snoring in a peaceful sleep. She tiptoed in and looked at his poor twisted face. She smiled at him, and the love in her eyes showed how much she thought of her big Granddaddy, as she'd always called him from almost the first the day she could talk.

And a big man he was too – close on 7 feet tall and a good 20 stone. Even now, at sixty-seven, it would be difficult to find more than 2 or 3 pounds of fat on him. He was broad, with powerful shoulders and arms, and very big hands. He had worked on the river nearly all his working life, from the age of twelve, most of the time as a lighterman. Everybody knew him as Big Alf. He was a great favourite with all, and he was always in the winning team when the barge races were on the go. It was said that he could handle a 200-ton barge like a rowing boat. He had even been picked to row the royal barge one year.

It was a sad day for everyone when, without warning, at the age of sixty-four he was suddenly struck by a severe stroke. At first he was completely paralysed down his left side, but slowly he managed to get back the use of his leg and most of the strength in his arm. His neck was stiff, and the left side of his face was twisted upwards, partly closing one eye and leaving his mouth gaping at the corner. There was no movement at all on this side of his face, making it difficult for him to talk. Now the only person who could always understand him was Betty – possibly because they were nearly inseparable. That's as it was always. He loved her from the moment he first set eyes on her. He had always wanted a daughter, but he had sired only sons – seven, to be exact.

Betty turned and crept from the room, gently closing the door behind her.

"He's sound asleep, Dad," she said as she entered her own room.

"I don't know how he does it, Betsy. It don't bother him at all. Now you can get into bed, love – mind all those bits on the floor in your bare feet. Oh, good! Here's Mum with a cuppa."

With Betty safely tucked up in bed, May and Sam slipped between the sheets, drank their tea, kissed and lay down to get some rest before it was time for work.

Before sleep had a chance to overtake them they were startled into a sitting position again by a loud knocking on the front door.

A man's voice called loudly, "Is there anybody in there?"

"What the bloody hell's up now?" cursed Sam as he put his feet to the floor and made his way to the window.

He drew back the curtains and lifted down the blackout frame. The knock came again as he forced up the bottom window.

"All right, all right, give us a chance, can't yer?"

He looked down into the street to see the warden with his white helmet pushed right to the back of his head looking up at him.

"Morning, Sam," he called in a tired voice. "I thought you might still be here."

"Wotcha, Bill," Sam replied. "What the hell d'you want, then?"

"You and your lot have got to get out and damn quick, Sam. The whole area's covered in unexploded bombs. There's three in this street; if you look at that telegraph pole over the road, you can see a bomb hanging from it. It could go off at any minute."

"Flaming hell!" said Sam.

The sight of the thing across the road made the small hairs on his neck stand on end.

"What shall we do?" he almost whispered to Bill below.

"Get down to the other end of the street and stay there till I come for you. Is there anybody next door?"

"I don't think so, Bill. The people at No. 25 sometimes don't go to the Tube, but this time I think I remember seeing them go."

"OK. Thanks, Sam. I'll just go and check. Now, look slippy."

In less than two minutes the four of them were making their

way towards the end of the street, picking their way over the rubble that in places almost blocked it altogether. Betty was holding tightly to Alf's big hand, as she always did when they were together.

Big Alf said something in his tortured voice.

May turned to her daughter and said, "What's your granddad say, Betty?"

"He said, 'It must have been some big raid to do all this damage. Half the street's missing.'"

"You're right," replied May, "and it's no thanks to you that we are still alive. We should have been in the Tube like most normal people was."

Sam quickly shut her up with a sharp "Leave it out, girl."

May flashed an angry look his way, but she shrugged her shoulders and said no more.

Betty looked at her granddad, smiled and squeezed his hand. He winked at her. They continued their way to the end of the street in silence.

Outside what was left of the Rose and Crown (it had been burnt out in one of the first air raids) there was a group of roughly twenty people. The Hawks family knew most of them by sight and one or two by name. They all knew Big Alf. He touched his cap as they said hello to him.

A man they all knew who lived in the next street, name of Wally, said to Sam, "Worst bugger we've had yet, isn't it, mate? My missus and me were bloody lucky. We just got in the shelter when the house just blew away and most of the street went with it. We had to dig our way out when it was all over. I kept thinking about you, mate. If I was you, I'd come down the Tube with us tonight."

"Don't you bleeding well start," said Sam.

"Oh, sorry, mate," Wally replied. "'ave yer been got at?" He nodded his head at May, who was looking the other way, and moved closer to Sam. Then, with his voice lowered, he went on: "We seem to be in a right two an' eight here, Sam. There don't seem to be any way out. The whole place is near wiped out. The only way open is down River End Road, but there's at least three unexploded bombs there. Anyway, here's the warden back. Did you find anybody up there, Bill?" He knew by the look on Bill's face what the answer would be.

Bill replied very quietly, "They're in there, Wally – all dead. They've been dead for hours, I should say, yet there's hardly a mark on them. It must have been the blast that did it."

They stood silent for a few minutes, then Wally said, more to himself than to anybody in particular, "This bloody, bloody war!"

Bill pulled himself together and called the men to one side. Their number amounted to just six, including Big Alf and Bill himself.

"Now, mates, when I was up the street I saw two more big ones, and there's a bomb slap in the middle of the road. I can't see why it didn't go off. It might have a delaying mechanism. Mind you, if it does go off it'll dislodge that one opposite your house, Sam, and that will go up with it. They'll flatten everything for half a mile. There's only one way out at the moment, but there's two bombs to get past first. There's another one lying in the road – you can see where it bounced along. I reckon that's a dud, but I can't be sure. A slight movement could set the bugger off.

There's another one up at the corner of the street. I saw its end sticking out of the wall of the fish shop. That's a time bomb for sure. You will have to walk right under it to get out – there's only a little passage left. The rubble's nearly 30 foot high there. Look – if you come to the corner, you can see what I mean."

They made their way to the corner, climbed on top of the bricks, floorboards, chimney pots and doors that had once been a house and peered up the road.

"Blimey, what a hell of a mess! It looks like it's burning well too. I can just make out what you're on about, Bill," said Sam.

The others nodded in agreement.

"Right, our best chance is to go out in small parties, each man taking three women or kids with him. All hold hands and go very slowly – and for Christ's sake be careful and don't make any noise. When you get through, give a wave; then I'll know you're clear. Make your way towards Commercial Road.

"You'd best go first, Harry, your wife being a cripple."

"All right, Bill, if you say so."

Harry turned and walked over to his missus.

"Come on, old girl – we're getting out of here. We're going up West for the day to see the King."

Everyone gave a shallow laugh at this, and those nearest helped Harry's wife to her feet and gave her her sticks.

She said, "See you all later."

They started on their way, Harry leading, his wife, their girl and the girl's friend making up the party.

"Right," said Bill, "The rest of you take cover behind the pub just in case they disturb anything on the way."

He made sure everybody had carried out his request before he ventured round the corner and climbed to the top of the rubble once more. From there he could watch Harry's progress, and he was mildly surprised at the distance the group had already covered. They were only about 12 feet from the first bomb. He saw Harry put his finger to his lips as they groped slowly past. It was another 100 yards to the fish shop. The fire was getting worse by the minute.

Suddenly, the roof of one of the houses fell in and Harry's party were showered with sparks and dust. They drew back and waited out of reach, they stopped for a few seconds, and Bill saw Harry take his coat off and put it over the head and shoulders of his wife. Then they moved off again, this time picking their way slowly along as near as they could to the wall.

Bill turned his head and called for Sam, who was quickly by his side.

"What's up, mate?" he asked.

11

"Look – that bloody fire's getting worse. We will have to look slippy. Go and get the next party sorted and tell them to get something to put over their heads and shoulders to protect them from the heat. When you hear me whistle, send the next party out," Bill said.

"OK, Bill," said Sam, and he was gone.

Harry had got past the fire, and Bill could dimly see them making their way quickly towards the bomb. As they moved slowly underneath that parcel of death, Bill held his breath, not knowing why, but possibly hoping it would help. They seemed to take ages before they were past. Bill blew out a long sigh of relief. He could just make out Harry through the smoke waving his coat above his head. He waved back and gave a long whistle.

Sam came forward with the next party, suitably dressed as per instructions. They went through nearly twice as quickly as the first group. The fire seemed neither better nor worse.

The next party were soon past the first bomb. They straggled past the fire. Just as they were 6 feet from the second bomb they stopped dead and looked up at it. The man leading them looked back at Bill and put his hand to his ear.

"My God," said Bill out loud, "the Bloody thing's started ticking."

He rose quickly to his feet and frantically waved them on.

The leader pushed his party in front of him. Two started to run, but the third tried to turn back. He got hold of her and started to drag her on. They seemed to fight. And then it was too late. Bill saw the fish shop and the end of the street heave into the air. He felt wind on his face. Then he never again felt anything.

As Sam and the rest of the party sat in the rubble behind the pub wall nobody had much to say. Most were feeling very tired after their night's ordeal. Big Alf was rolling a smoke; Betty sat across one of his knees, resting against his big chest.

Sam said, "It will soon be our turn to be off, girl."

His wife just nodded and gave him a weak smile. He had just opened his mouth to speak to Alf when a giant hand picked him up and sent him sprawling over the rubble 20 feet away. Then he heard the explosion and felt bricks, etc. raining down on him. He covered his head with his arms and just lay there struggling to get his breath, waiting for it to stop.

After what seemed an age, all went quiet. He opened his eyes and peered about. The air was thick with dust, the sun shining through it. Sam moved his arms – all right – then his legs. They seemed all right too, but the right one was held down. He looked at it and saw that it was trapped by the old pub window frame and about 200 bricks. He remembered the others and called, "May, May, are you all right, girl?"

May's weak voice replied, "I think so, Sam, but I can't move for damn bricks."

Sam called out, "Dad, are you and Betty OK?"

He heard Alf s deep voice say something, and almost at once Betty said with a trembling voice close to tears, "Granddaddy says we are OK and keep still and he will get you out."

Soon strong hands were throwing aside bricks, then Alf got a grip on the frame and lifted it enough for Sam to get free. Betty was pulling bricks from her mother. In no time the whole party were freed. By some miracle nobody was badly hurt. Although the wall had fallen on top of them, no doubt it had saved their lives. Many of them had bad cuts and plenty of bruises.

Alf said something to Sam, and little Betty translated: "He says he's going to look for Bill and that bomb must have gone off."

"All right. Be careful," said Sam.

The old man moved with incredible agility over the rubble towards where Bill had been. It was difficult to tell what was what. The corner of the street was no longer recognisable. Alf climbed up as far as he dared on the unstable mess and looked in the direction of where the fish shop and the end of the street had been. He just couldn't believe it: there was nothing there to tell him where either had been. The only familiar thing was the fire, which now seemed to be everywhere and rapidly spreading. He wondered where the other bomb was, and how long it would be before the fire got to it. Then it too would go off.

Of Bill there was no sign. Alf tried to gauge where he might have been blown, but without success. He turned and started to make his way back. Then, while clambering over a large wooden beam, he saw something white and red out of the corner of his eye, below him and to the right. He pulled at the timber and bricks until he was able to reach down and grab what he thought was Bill's first-aid kit – the bag with the red cross on it. He took it back to the others, and May set to and used it to tend some of the injured heads and bodies.

Alf told them, through Betty, what he had seen.

"You mean there's no way out that way, and we are trapped here with all those bloody bombs liable to go off at any damn time."

Sam could feel himself starting to tremble as the words came from his mouth. His face was twitching. He knew he was on the verge of blind panic. He heard his voice start to rise.

Then two big hands fell on his shoulders and shook him until his teeth rattled in his jaw. A voice whispered in his ear, and, although he could not understand the words, he knew only too well their meaning: "Shut yer face or I'll belt yer."

His father had always done that when he misbehaved.

Sam soon pulled himself together, hung his head and said, "Sorry."

May put her arm round him, and, with tears running into her mouth, she blazed at her father-in-law: "You're such a clever sod! How the hell do you think we are gonna get out, then?"

She buried her head in Sam's neck. Betty had started to cry

14

and so had two of the other women. Alf stood up, got hold of Betty's hand, and faced them. He seemed to have grown a foot taller. He looked a fearsome sight; with his mouth trying to shape words they could understand, his saliva dripped from his mouth and down the front of his coat and he blew spit in all directions.

"Shut up!" he bellowed with such ferocity that they immediately became quiet.

They held their breath and looked at him in horror.

Words began to pour from his mouth, and he paused to see if they had understood. When he saw that they had not, he gently shook Betty's arm and waved his other arm towards them. She shook her head from side to side. Alf shook her a bit harder, waved his arm again and said something to her. May started to go towards her. Sam held her tight and shook his head.

Betty looked at them and said, "Granddaddy said we are to stop acting like kids. Maybe we are trapped at the moment, but grizzling isn't going to help."

She stopped and looked up at Big Alf, waiting for his next words. He blurted out his message, talking more to her now than to the others. When he had finished she paused, looking into his face as if trying to understand properly.

"Are you sure, Granddaddy? You're not just saying that?"

He ignored her enquiry and just waved his hand at the others.

Betty turned to them. "He says he knows a way out, but we must go now – but carefully."

At first nobody moved. They were all thinking, 'What does this old fool know?'

Alf sensed this, and so did Betty.

She said, "My Granddaddy knows everything about the dock and the river." She turned from them. "I am ready, Granddaddy."

He lifted her up on to his massive shoulders and started to move across the rubble away from where the pub had stood. The rest of the party suddenly felt they did not want to be left behind. They were ready to follow any leader. They crossed two or three gardens until they came to what had once been a high brick wall but was now a heap of bricks. Alf stood still for a good minute or more, looking this way and that, trying to get his bearings. He then set off to the right, moving parallel to the wall between two trees, one of which looked as if it had been struck by lightning. Alf moved to where the wall stood tall and sound. He looked over and said something to Betty.

She joined him and said, "I can't see much but damage. What's it look like?"

Alf said something more, and Betty looked again.

Then she pointed and said, "There's part of an iron railing on the other side of the big heap of rubble there."

Alf nodded and moved on to the next break in the wall, where he made his way through. On top of a heap of bricks he looked about again. He said something to Betty, and she scrambled back to the others and said, "Granddaddy says he wants Dad to go with him and we are to stay here until they get back."

Sam made his way to his father's side and said, "What's up, then?"

Alf pointed forward and slightly to the right. At first all Sam could see were rubble and fires as far as it was possible to see. Alf took his arm and pointed again, making circles and pointing to the ground. It was a bit beyond Sam; he wondered about his father. Alf shrugged his shoulders and waved his hand in disgust; then he motioned Sam to follow him. He also pointed to Sam's eyes, moving his arm around in front of him, and made a noise that Sam took to mean 'bombs'.

"Keep my eyes open for bombs?" he said.

Alf nodded and moved forward, picking his way through the devastation. Sam followed behind, continually looking about. After 200 yards they moved into what was once a small street. He could see patches of pavement here and there. The thought crossed his mind that he should know it well as he had lived hereabouts all his life; and yet it was so different. Nothing was recognisable. It was like being in a different world.

"I don't know how the hell you can possibly know where we are," he called to his father. "It's like being on the bloody moon."

Alf said nothing, but he picked his way steadily forward, every now and again stopping and looking this way and that. Sam watched him for a few seconds. 'He's like a bloodhound searching about,' he thought. 'It beats me if I know what the hell he's looking for.'

They rounded a larger than normal mountain of destruction to be confronted by a double-decker bus. It was tilted on one side with its wheels at least 3 feet off the ground. Oil and water were still dripping from the engine. All the windows on the side they could see were unbroken. Alf stood looking at it and then made his way to the front. Sam saw him look up at the destination plate: '10A Tooting Broadway' it said.

"What the hell's that doing round here?" questioned Sam.

He turned to his father and saw that he was not going to get an answer. The look of horror in his eyes made Sam look again at the front of the bus. This time he saw it: sitting bolt upright, still clutching the steering wheel, was the driver. He was wearing his white summer hat and coat, but he had no face.

Sam felt his stomach come up past his tonsils. He turned away and he was violently sick.

After a few minutes he felt his father's hand on his shoulder and he blurted out something that sounded like "Come on, Sam."

He wiped his mouth and followed on behind. Somewhere ahead rubber was burning, and thick black smoke was drifting towards them. After another 100 yards they could see what it was: amongst piles of rubble a fire engine was burning fiercely from end to end.

Big Alf paused here and looked about him.

"You're bloody lost, old man, like me," said Sam.

Alf looked at his son sharply, but Sam was right.

17

A few minutes later the wind changed direction slightly and the black smoke drifted to the left of them. Another smell took its place, and Sam saw his father's face light up.

"That's the sewer vent up . . ." His voice trailed off as the full significance of his words came to him. "Blimey, Dad! If we could find that, at least we would know where we are."

They set off with more enthusiasm, and in five minutes they had located it. The steel pipe was missing, but the door and the brickwork were free from damage. Alf approached the door, turned the handle and gave it a hard tug. It never moved.

"Christ Almighty, isn't there enough smell without opening the door?"

Alf looked at his son and started to say something, but he thought better of it, got down on one knee and motioned for Sam to do the same. He cleared a patch on the ground, and, with a piece of wood, Alf drew what at first looked like a snake. Then he wrote 'river' next to it and waved his arm in the general direction of the Thames.

"Right, that's the river," said Sam.

The old man then draw a square, put 'S' in it and pointed to the vent.

"Right," said Sam doubtfully.

His father then drew two lines from the square to the river, walked his fingers along it and looked at his son.

"You mean we can get along the sewer to the river. That's a bloody good idea, mate. But wait a minute – you'll never be able to go down there with your claustrophobia. You can't even go on the Tube."

The old man's head hung down, his face trembled and the sweat poured from his forehead; then he quickly got to his feet and motioned Sam to go back for the others.

Alf searched about for something big and heavy, and he came back with an iron gatepost, with which he attacked the sewer door. The thing was good and strong, but it was no match for this giant of a man with the determination of ten men. Before Sam got back it was off its hinges and lying to one side.

Alf sat down and mopped his brow.

'It's damn hot for the time of year,' he thought.

In no time the others were coming into sight. Alf got to his feet.

Betty found her granddad's hand, and, looking up into his face, said, "Ain't it blooming awful, Granddaddy?"

He nodded and spoke two or three words to her.

She looked at her father and said, "Granddaddy said we can have a little rest before going in and will you tell everybody what we are going to do?"

Sam nodded, looked at the others and, in his pronounced Cockney lingo, proceeded to tell them of his father's plans.

At first the women in the party were horrified at the thought, and May soon informed everyone in no uncertain terms that nobody was going to get her down no bloody sewer.

"Well, if that's the way yer feels about it, girl, you'll just have to stay here; but for your information, just back there by that bus we passed there's a bloody great bomb which just might go off at any moment."

The women looked at one another.

"Is there no other way out anywhere?" one enquired of Big Alf.

He looked thoughtful before blurting out his reply, which Betty translated as "There more than likely is, but we don't know where and we don't know what we might disturb in trying to find one. At least there won't be a lot of rubble down in the sewer, so we should be able to get along better. I know it leads to the river, and once we get there we'll be all right."

There was a short pause as the women pondered this point.

"Well," said May, "I suppose it must be better than sitting here with a bomb, and what's more—"

She stopped as from the distance they all clearly heard the siren warning everyone to take cover.

"Bleeding hell!" let out Sam in anger. "Them bastards are coming back again."

Everyone was back on their feet again, and they all looked at Big Alf. He looked at Betty and said something. She moved to her mother's side and felt in the Red Cross bag she still carried. She brought out a torch and switched it on.

"It works all right, Granddaddy," she said.

He took it from her outstretched hand and headed for the door. Here he stopped and looked round at them all, then at the sky. Sam could see the sweat glistening on his face.

He moved up beside his father and whispered, "Go on, mate – you can do it. You're the only one – for the kid's sake."

Alf shot him a quick glance, felt for Betty's hand and again mumbled his message to her through his twisted face.

"Keep close together and one behind the other," Betty whispered in a frightened, trembling voice.

They moved forward through the door and began to descend the steps. After the bright sunshine outside it seemed pitch-black beyond the faint beam of torchlight. As they worked their way slowly down, they became more used to their new environment. The smell at first choked them, but as they got deeper and deeper the air became fresher. It also got colder.

After descending about 30 feet Betty's voice echoed, "Careful! The steps are slippery here, but we are nearly at the bottom."

Another ten or twelve steps found them standing on a small concrete platform with running water about 4 feet below them. Sam remarked that, judging by marks on the walls, the water was a good 2 feet lower than it sometimes was. The water was quite clear, slow-running and only 6 inches deep.

"I suppose", remarked May, "it's low because nobody is using the drains."

Sam nodded in agreement.

A muffled 'vamp-vamp' drifted down from the open door through which they had just come.

Somebody said, "Here they come," and the group moved forward again along a 2-foot-wide path just above the high-water level.

Here they were forced to walk in a crouched position. After 200 yards or so they became aware of a sound like a waterfall, and a little further on they saw water cascading down from an opening on their left.

"Blimey!" said Sam. "I reckon that's a burst water main. Which way do we go?"

Alf's arm went up, indicating the other side of the waterfall.

Betty piped up, "I wish I had brought my swimsuit, Mum."

The merriment in her voice caused a ripple of amusement to run through the party, but this was quickly replaced by moans as they were forced to step into the cold water to get past the waterfall. Most were pretty wet by the time they got back on to the path again.

Soon the tunnel widened and the water became a lot deeper. Then, after another 300 yards, the tunnel sloped sharply downwards for about 12 feet.

At the bottom of this slope they found themselves in a new tunnel, a good 12 to 14 feet wide. Alf stopped and shone the torch in both directions. He muttered something to Betty.

"What, Granddaddy?" she asked.

After a pause, he spoke again.

"Granddaddy says this is the main that goes straight to the river, but he says something is wrong: the water's too high and he doesn't think it's the tide."

Sam said, "If it's not the tide, then perhaps there's a blockage somewhere between us and the river. Judging by the way the water's rising, that seems the most likely explanation."

Betty said, "Granddaddy says you're right, Dad. We will have to go a different way. He says there's another tunnel."

They all turned and passed over a little bridge to a path on the other side of the flowing water. They hurried along, and Alf led with the torch.

After a good twenty minutes, Betty said, "Is it much further Granddaddy? I'm blooming tired and cold."

Sam said, "Come to me, love. I'll carry you for a bit."

"No," came the sharp reply, "I'm staying with Granddaddy."

Alf lifted her up on to his shoulders again and said something in answer to her question which satisfied her but puzzled everybody else.

Another 50 yards or so further on they came to a flight of sixty steps, which led up to a smaller tunnel. Here there was no path, but no water either. At first it was very steep, but it levelled out after a short distance and became just a gentle upward slope. Sam was bringing up the rear of the party.

Suddenly they heard what sounded like a Tube train coming from behind them.

"Get down, everybody! Get down quick!" Sam shouted, and he threw himself on top of May.

As they hit the tunnel floor together, a fierce wind blew over them followed by a roaring sound. It soon passed away, but left them coughing and spluttering in the dust and fumes that blew about them.

"What the hell was that?" somebody said.

"A bomb must have gone off in the main somewhere. It's a good job we got out of it when we did," Sam answered.

There was a quick movement, a few squeaks, and a scream from Betty as a family of very wet rats rushed by them up the tunnel.

"I hate this rotten place," half screamed May, near to panic.

"Steady on, old girl!" said Sam. Then, calling ahead to Big Alf,

22

he went on: "How much further do you reckon it is, then?"

Alf mumbled something to Betty.

"Granddaddy says about another 200 yards further the tunnel gets smaller, then after another 50 yards there's a door."

"Good! Let's go, then," said Sam in reply, and they all shuffled forward again.

Sure enough, after 200 yards they came to a small room-like area with three other tunnels leading from it. Two were little more than 2 feet in diameter; the third was 4 feet.

Betty relayed Alf's words as he lifted her down from his shoulders: "We have got to crawl along this, but it is dry."

Sam pondered this. Why were all the tunnels dry? They looked as if they had never had water in them at all. There were lots of cobwebs about.

Soon the procession stopped again. Sam got the message that they had arrived at the door but could not get it open – would he try to find something to help break it down with?

'Where the hell does he think I'm going to get something like that from down here?' Sam said to himself.

Out loud he said, "OK."

He turned round, brought out his lighter and started back down the tunnel, searching this way and that as he went. He reached the little 'room' without finding anything. He straightened up and looked about him. Then his eye caught sight of a small handrail at the entrance to the tunnel through which they had first come, and he remembered feeling it was loose when he had leant against it. He went to it and gave it a mighty pull with his free hand. One end came away from the wall. He pulled again. The other end twisted about but stayed bolted in position. Sam put the lighter in his pocket and took hold of the rail in both hands. He twisted, turned and pulled until the rusty bolts broke and the rail came away altogether. He made his way back into the 4-foot tunnel and started to crawl along towards the others.

Suddenly he heard May's voice calling him: "Sam, Sam, for God's sake hurry up! Your old man's not feeling too well."

Sam crawled faster and shouted, "All right, all right, I'm coming. I've got something. Don't panic – I'm coming."

When he reached the others May whispered, "He's feeling the effects of being shut up in this small tunnel. You go to him, Sam."

Sam squeezed past the rest of the party and made his way to his father's side. Big Alf was bathed in sweat, his eyes were staring and his big frame was shaking violently from head to foot as he lay on the floor of the tunnel. Noises were coming from his twisted face. Betty was beside him, holding one big hand in hers.

With tears flowing down her face, she sobbed, "It's all right, Granddaddy. We'll soon have you out now."

Sam said, "Come on, mate – let's get this bastard door down. Here, Betty, you hold the torch."

She shone it on the door, which was little more than 3 feet square – not so much a door, but wooden planks put up to block the entrance into the sewage system.

Sam attacked it at the base, where it looked rotten – and so it proved to be, for the first blow with the rail went right through the wood. In less than three minutes the way was clear.

Sam took the torch and went through the opening, but he was confronted by a brick wall only 4 feet away. He stood up and shone the torch about, and there, only 2 feet above him, was a manhole cover. He pushed at it with the rail and was showered with dirt and rust.

"Blimey, that bugger's solid!" he said out loud, and he was aware of Betty pulling at his trouser leg. "What's up, girl?" he asked.

Back came the answer: "Granddaddy says he knows how to open it."

Sam wormed his way back into the tunnel and Alf squeezed into the small space below the manhole. For a full ten minutes Alf heaved, strained and cursed, and then a sigh was heard followed by a draught of warmer musty air. The next fifteen minutes were taken up with getting the whole party up through the hole.

When all were safely on their feet, Sam looked about him. He was on the point of saying, "Where the hell are we?" when May said, "Well, I'm blowed! We've come up in a Gents lavvy. Blimey – now I've seen everything!" She half laughed.

Sam moved round the tiled wall towards the door. The rest followed. Greatly to their surprise they found themselves on a Tube-station platform.

"Well, bugger me!" exclaimed Sam. "It's a Tube station."

Alf said something to Betty, who turned to everybody and said, "Anybody got a match, then?"

Somebody gave her a box, which she in turn gave to Alf. He lit a candle that was on a small ledge in the wall. It was the remains of a big church candle and gave a fair old light.

Sam thought, 'He's been here before. He knew that was there. I wonder how.'

"How do we get out, then?" asked one of the women. "I'm dying for a cuppa."

Betty again translated Alf's message: "This part of the Tube was built in eighteen hundred and something, but water seeped in from the river so they never used it. They bricked it up at both ends. The only route out of here is through the air duct. Once we have had a rest, we'll have a go at it."

Alf sat down on the floor with his back to the tiled wall. Betty went to her mother and whispered, "I want a wee, Mum."

"Yes, so do I, love," May whispered back. "Sam, let's have that torch while we find the Ladies."

When the women had all gone in, Sam sat down by his old man.

"You've been here before, ain't you?" he asked, looking into the old man's face.

Alf nodded yes, but made no sign of wanting to reveal where or when.

Sam went on: "Where's this air duct, then, and where does it come out?"

Alf pointed to the other end of the platform, and then wrote in the dust between them, 'It comes out by the river.'

There was a lot more that Sam would have liked to know, but Alf was saying no more.

After some twenty minutes Alf got to his feet and walked to the end of the platform and into a small room. He moved to a grille at the back wall, and, after a bit of pushing and pulling, lifted it free from its supports and placed it on the tiled floor. This revealed a 3-foot-square air duct made of steel, which tapered in. Alf motioned the others to get ready.

Betty said, "Granddaddy says we will have to be careful at the other end in case the way out has been damaged, and maybe the raid's still on." She looked at her father and went on: "Will you bring the bar with you for breaking down doors just in case we need it?"

Sam nodded his reply and went to fetch the rail from the Gents, where he had left it. On the way back to the others he stopped in front of the lighted candle, looking at the 2 inches yet to burn. 'It's a good job you were still there,' he thought. 'I'll put you out in case someday somebody else should need you.'

He took his lighter from his pocket, lit it and blew out the candle.

He passed a door that he had not noticed before, and something made him stop and turn back. He tried the door handle, but it was locked. He held the lighter closer to the door, and it was then that he noticed one pane of glass was missing. He put his arm through the space and the lighter lit up the interior of the small white-tiled room. There was an old round-bottomed chair standing against one wall and a tea chest standing upside down had been used as a table. The wall facing the door had two pipes running across it. The bottom one had two pieces of rope hanging from it about 4 feet apart. The pipe was bent as if it had once supported a great weight. Near the floor the tiles had been broken and some were missing. There were splashes of something on the walls.

'Funny!' thought Sam. 'I wonder why that's locked.'

As he turned to go, Betty's voice echoed, "Dad, are you coming?"

"Yes, I'm on my way, love," Sam answered.

He moved to where the others were waiting and said, "There's another little room back there."

Before he could say any more Alf flashed him a look and shook his head. Sam got the message and shut up.

Alf waved his arm towards the air duct and lifted Betty up into it. He said something to her.

"All right," she said, and, taking the torch, she started up the shaft.

Alf eased himself into the opening, but remained there.

Betty's voice could be heard from a distance: "Coo, it ain't 'alf steep! And it's all broken here."

Alf could hear her struggling, and her tortured breath worried him. He called to her, and her breathless reply did nothing to reassure him.

"I'm nearly stuck, Granddaddy. It goes round a corner and straight up."

He shouted back to her, and there was a short silence while everybody strained their ears.

"OK. I have found it." There was another short pause, broken by a yell. "It's broke and I hurt me knee." Alf hurriedly said something to her, and she said, "OK."

A few minutes later she appeared in the opening and Alf lifted her down into the room. May ran to her.

"Are you all right, love?" she enquired.

Betty in reply pointed to her injured knee.

"I cut it when the rope broke."

May proceeded to dress the wound. Alf said something to her. She held up her hands.

"Straight up. Yes, it's rotten, I reckon."

Alf thought for a few minutes then started to remove his belt and spluttered his instructions.

Betty sighed a little and said, "Granddaddy wants things we can make a rope with, like belts, stockings, coats – anything like that."

Off came belts, coats and other pieces of clothing. Alf proceeded to make them into a long 'rope'. With this done, he issued further instructions through Betty.

"Granddaddy and I are going to try to get up this steep bit. He is going to tie the rope round his feet so that he can help you up. Once we are over that, we are as good as out."

So in Betty went again. This time Alf went with her. The two worked their way around the bend, and Alf managed to push Betty up the tall chimney and then, through sheer brute strength, he forced himself up too. He then secured the 'rope' and shouted to them to come up one at a time.

This took the best part of an hour, and it was getting hot in the confined space. Sam wondered how his old man was enduring being confined in such a small space. The funny thing was that he seemed to be coping better now than when he was in the Tube.

Betty asked if she could go on, and Alf said, "OK, but be careful."

She set off, taking the torch with her. The others set off after her.

Their sore hands and knees had gone another 30 yards when they heard a cry from Betty: "I can see daylight! I can see the end and I can smell the river. It's a long way, but it's lovely."

The others sighed and laughed a little at her excitement. It gave them new encouragement to force their tortured bodies forward.

Soon they could all see the light and smell the fresh river air.

They were able to get to their feet and stumble along the last 20 feet to where a wooden slatted grille barred their way. Sam looked through and remarked that there was a lot of rubble about, but not enough to block the entrance entirely.

The trusty handrail once again came into its own. This time a bit more hard work was required than before, but between them Alf and Sam managed to force a way through.

A few minutes later there they stood, leaning up against the rubble in the afternoon sun with a cool breeze from the river blowing over them like champagne. Nobody spoke as they enjoyed it. Sam looked at them and could scarcely believe his eyes. There were eight of them including himself. His father, with his face turned towards the river, had one hand in his pocket, helping to keep his trousers up. His shirt was torn to shreds. The flesh showed through the skin on top of his left shoulder, and congealed blood stained his forearm. The knees were out of his trousers, and cuts could be seen in his big kneecaps. His twisted face, like the rest of him, was covered in thick grime, through which rivers of sweat still ran. But still he looked fantastically powerful.

Next to him, as usual holding his hand, sat Betty with her chin on her chest, looking at the torch in her hand. Sam was not quite sure if she was nearly in tears or asleep. Her hair was matted with grime and cobwebs. Her nightdress had split from the neck to near the waist, and it hung down on one shoulder, leaving her chest bare. She was covered in dirt and scratches. Around her left knee were the dirty remains of the bandage May had fixed up for her. She had no socks, and one strap of her school sandals was broken.

'Poor kid!' Sam thought to himself. 'I bet she's buggered.'

His gaze moved to his wife, May. She stood in the sun with her head back and her eyes closed as if she might never have the chance of soaking it up again. She too was covered in grime from head to foot. Her nightdress was badly torn, but it was held together by the strap of the Red Cross bag she still carried. She had no stockings on, and her best shoes, with the toes nearly worn out through crawling, were beyond repair.

The other four women were in much the same state: dirty, torn and battered nearly beyond recognition. The oldest of them, a small thin women, stood with her hands in her lap looking straight at Alf, and the tears were cascading from her brown eyes down through the dirt on her face.

Sam felt moved. He shifted his tired, near-naked body close to her side, put his arm around her shoulders and said softly, "There, now, girl! There's no need to cry now. It's nearly all over."

"I know, I know," she sobbed, "and it's all thanks to that lovely Big Alf. If it 'adn't been for him, we'd all been goners. Ain't that true?"

She looked at the other women about her, and May looked from the woman's tear-stained face to Alf.

"By God, you're right, mate! He's a bloody marvel. He brought us up from hell, and no mistake."

She went to Alf's side and kissed his twisted face. Alf put his arm round her. Sam felt like bursting into tears then, it being the first time he could ever remember May saying a good word to or about his old man. It was a very emotional moment as all the women came forward and kissed Big Alf.

He reminded them that they were not out of the woods yet, and he instructed them to stay put while he and Sam went and had a look round.

The air duct had come out on a piece of waste ground near a dock.

Sam remarked that he had passed it hundreds of times and had not even known what was there. They climbed over the rubble, and Sam remarked, "It's a good job the tide's in; let's go and find a boat."

Off came their boots, and in a flash he and Alf were in the

water, swimming towards the basin entrance. As they entered the river properly they could just make out the all-clear sounding in the distance. Sam caught his father's eye and gave him a thumbs-up.

Twenty yards on, Sam saw a rope leading from a small jetty into the water. He took a deep breath and dived down to look. Sure enough, there was a small rowing boat floating just under the surface. It had been swamped by a big wave caused by a bomb falling in the river. He told his father, and together they soon had it floating on top with very little water in it. Alf climbed in, stood up and looked about for the missing oars. Luckily, one was bobbing up and down against the dock wall not far away; the other was some way away, but it was found to be broken. Sam retrieved the good one and was pulled aboard the boat by his father.

In no time they where back at the basin, where they picked up the others, and then they headed upriver on the tide.

"We'd best make for the other side by Tower Bridge," Sam remarked to his father as they approached the centre of the river.

May called out, "Look! Look over there! There's some people. Look – they're waving." She waved back. "Ain't it nice to see people again!"

At Tower Bridge they couldn't find a landing place, so they agreed to go further upriver.

"Blimey, just look at London Bridge! That's taken a belting."

"Oh, what a shame!" said one of the women.

Sam went on: "We can land over there. Look – by the bridge, where those people are waving."

They manoeuvred the boat across, and as soon as it touched the side eager hands went out to them, helping them out and throwing blankets round their near-naked bodies. They were virtually carried to the first-aid post at the back of Southwark Cathedral.

The next four or five hours were a blur of activity. For what seemed like days, they were washed, examined, inspected and asked thousands of questions, most of which they were unable to answer. They were moved from here to there, given clothes and a meal, and handed cups of tea everywhere they went. After a journey by bus they were put into a big room and so to bed, and that's the last thing most of them remembered for nearly twelve hours.

But, like a lot of Londoners, they would never forget 7–9 September 1940, the nights when London burnt, when close on 850 souls were killed, 2,500 were injured, and thousands of others lost friends and neighbours, their homes and often almost everything they owned.

* * * * *

Big Alf, Sam, May and Betty were moved two or three times, and in the end they were put on a train for Westmorland. In other words, they were evacuated. They were lucky to be still all together.

After they had been settled in for a week Sam had a chance to talk to his father alone, and this was something he had been bursting to do. Armed with a notepad and pencil he asked the questions that had been eating him ever since their escape.

"What I want to know is how the hell did you know that Tube station was there? And how did you know you could get there from the sewer?"

The old man sat there, not moving, pulling deep on his home-made cigarette as if he had not heard a word Sam had said. A dark expression crept over his twisted face, and a shudder passed through his big frame as if he had been stung by an icy wind, but still he made no movement.

Sam said, "Come on – you've got to tell me something. May's

already asking about it, and it might not be long before it dawns on Betty that you knew all the time the place was there."

At this Alf turned his head towards Sam and looked at him hard with his good eye. Slowly his head went up and down. He reached for the pad and pencil and started to write:

'What I'm going to tell you, boy, is the truth, but you must never tell a living soul.'

He looked at Sam, who read what was written and said, "OK, I'll not tell anybody, I promise."

Alf once again looked deeply at his son before continuing to write:

'It all started a long, long time ago, back in the 1860s, when my old man (your grandfather) was in his thirties. It was a bloody hard life in them days. He worked as a docker, and when he started loading or unloading a ship he kept going until it was finished. He was paid 2 shillings a load, which sometimes took three days and nights. It must have been a hell of a struggle when he got married and babies came along.

'Well, one day my dad and two or three of his mates were unloading tea on the East Indian Dock. The Captain wanted a quick turnround so he put the ship's bosun in charge of the job. Well, this upset the bosun's shore-leave plans, and he was determined to take his frustration out on someone. My father was a big bloke, like me, so the bosun picked on a smaller bloke. In those days all bosuns carried a small truncheon or a knotted rope called a starter. Well, he kept on at this little man until in his hurry he dropped a chest back down into the hold and it split open.

'This was just what the bosun was waiting for, and he laid in to the little bloke with such fury that he knocked him into the hold. The old man dropped everything and went down and got him out with the help of some of his mates. The bosun was bellowing for them to get back to work, and as soon as they reached the deck he set about them with his starter. The old man told him to pack it in or he'd take the rope off him. By this time the bosun was completely out of control, and he turned to bring his starter down on the old man's head. My father just moved to one side, plastered him one on the chin, took the starter and threw it overboard into the river. The bosun struggled to his feet, took hold of a hatch iron and went for him. My father backed off and warned him that if he came near him he would throw him into the river. The bosun raised the iron above his head and attempted to split the old man's head open. My father took a step towards him, grabbed the iron in one hand and the man's belt in the other, lifted the bosun above his head and threw him and the iron into the water amid cheers and laughter from his mates.

'The trouble was that the whole thing had been witnessed by the Captain, who now ordered the gang off his ship. So there they were, nearly a full day's work put in and no pay. By the next day most had found other ships to work on, but the word had got round that my father was a troublemaker. Nobody would employ him, and so it went on for weeks.'

The old man paused, looked at Sam, then drank deep from the glass of beer his son had poured for him. He wiped his mouth with the back of his hand and started to write again. Sam read the words as they were formed.

'My old man was getting desperate. Nobody was willing to take him on, and there was no food in the house. All sorts of things were going through his mind. Although he was a big man, the thought of holding up some seaman just ashore filled him with horror; but one night he left the house at ten o'clock with just that thought in mind.

'Soon he was walking along the dockside. Some boats were being worked on, but not many. He made his way, keeping to the shadows, towards a spot where not much was going on, and he stood concealed in a warehouse doorway. From there he could see three of four ships moored in the river and also the road leading from the dock. After keeping watch for nearly thirty minutes he was about to move when he heard voices. Three men were coming down the road towards the dock. He watched them come towards him, and his interest grew when they slowed to a stop no more than 15 feet away.

'The shortest of the three whispered, "Now, you know what you've got to do. As soon as he turns up I'll go towards him and start chatting. You come from behind and let him have it. Then get the stuff and away. If there is any trouble, split up and meet at my place in the morning. Now get over there out of sight. It won't be long before he's here."

'The two men disappeared into the shadows opposite where my old man stood. The other concealed himself just outside the circle of light from a gas lamp on the wall no more than 10 feet away.

'Fifteen minutes elapsed before the sound of a boat being rowed ashore from a big passenger ship anchored in the river could be heard. It knocked against the dock wall and footsteps echoed up the stone steps. A medium-built seaman with a large beard stepped on to the dockside.

'He was dressed in the uniform of a chief steward. He stood there for a few minutes, looking about him, then took off his peaked cap and mopped his brow with a white handkerchief. After replacing the cap he took a pipe and baccy pouch from his tunic pocket, tapped the pipe on the heel of his shiny black shoes, filled the pipe from the pouch and lit it. Only when it was well alight and the smoke was billowing up in the still night air did he take a leisurely step forward. He slowly walked towards the road, and when he was nearly at the dock entrance the little man stepped into the circle of light and started walking towards him. The bearded man saw him as soon as he moved, but made no sign of recognition.

'"Pardon me, sir. I would be most grateful if you could supply me with a light for my cigar."

'The bearded one reached in his pocket and threw a box of matches towards the advancing figure.

'"Keep them, Jock," he said, and he moved to one side to avoid the man in front of him.

'My old man saw the other two coming fast from behind, and before he could stop himself he shouted out, "Look out behind, mate."

'The bearded man sprang forward like a cat and caught the first man square on the chin. He slumped to the ground, but another of the men brought an iron bar crashing down on top of him, doing a lot of damage. The third man was taking a weapon from his pocket when my old man picked him up and hurled him head first into the wall, where he ceased to move. His huge fist came down on the neck of the man with the bar, who was doing his best to make pulp of the bearded man's face, and the man rolled into the road and was still. All was quiet. The old man took a quick look round – nobody seemed to be about.

'A quick search through all their pockets and away, he thought.

'He looked at the bearded one. Blood was gushing from the wound in his head.

'"Blimey, mate, you're gonna die if I leave you."

'So saying, he picked him up over one shoulder like a baby, and in a split second he was in the boat rowing to the boat the bearded man had come from.

'"Ahoy there!" shouted the old man.

'Almost immediately came an answer: "Who is it?"

'"I have got your chief steward here and he's hurt bad."

'Soon willing hands were helping them aboard.

'Someone said, "Get the old man," meaning the Captain.

'"Quick!" said a broad Scots voice. "Put him in my cabin. Right, steward, towels and hot water, man! The rest of you, get back to your duties at the double."

'As soon as they were alone, the Captain said, "Now, man,

before anybody comes back tell me what happened."

'While my old man was giving him the low-down he was stripping the steward's tunic and shirt off. Underneath was a leather body belt; this he took off and quickly put into a drawer.

'"You've never seen that, laddie, do you ken?"

'"Oh, yes, governor," came the reply.

'The steward came in with the hot water.

'"Put it over there, and give this man a double tot of my best."

'"Aye aye, sir," said the steward, and he pushed a glass into my father's hand.

'"Now get out. I'll send for you if I need you."

'The Captain was busy with the first-aid box, cleaning up the chief steward.

'"My God! I do believe he has a broken arm as well. No doubt if you had not come along they would have killed him and got what they came for."

As the Captain finished the bandaging, the bearded man started to moan.

'"Give me that bottle, man, and hold him up while I get some of this into him."

'He forced the liquid between the man's swollen lips. The chief steward drank and then coughed half of it back up.

'"Drink it, Robby. Blast you, drink it!"

'The man did as he was told and then opened one eye and took in his surroundings.

'"Did they—?" he started.

'"No," broke in the Captain. "Thanks to this man, they didn't wipe you out either."

'Robby turned his eye and took in the stranger.

'"Thanks, mate," he said.

'"All right, mate. I'm glad I was there."

'The Captain opened the door and yelled. The steward came running.

'"Take Mr Roberts to his cabin."

'"Aye aye, sir."

'The Captain moved to the table, kicked a chair round and motioned my old man to sit down. He filled the empty glass my father was still holding in his hand and then his own glass.

'"What's your name?"

'"John – Big John, Captain."

'"Aye, you're big all right. Here's your very good health, John. You have done me a great favour this night and no mistake. Well, drink up, man – do you no like rum? It's the best."

'"Oh, yes, Captain, I likes it fine, but on an empty gut it makes me feel sick."

'"Why, is it that long since you last ate?"

'"Nearly three days, Captain."

'"I'll soon fix that, lad."

'At the door he yelled for the steward, and in five minutes John was getting himself the right side of soup with bread, butter and cheese.

'The Captain said, "Eat your fill, Big John."

'He said no more until my father had finished. He just sat there, watching him and knocking back the rum. My father could tell that all the time he was weighing him up, trying to make up his mind about him.

'When he had finished, he thanked the Captain and added, "I hope the chief steward will be all right, sir."

'"Oh, aye, Big John. He's tough and will mend well. Now tell me why a big, strong man like you has not enough to feed himself. What's your job?"

'John told him and explained why he could not get work on the dock.

'The Captain chuckled a bit at the story and then said, "Now, Big John, how would you like to work for me?"

'"Well, Captain, I know all about boats and the river better than most men, but I ain't even seen the sea. I'm no sailor."

'The Captain held up his hand. "No, no, John – I have plenty of seamen. I want you to work for me ashore."

'"I'll do anything, Captain – anything so that I can feed the wife and kids."

'"All I want you to do is to get things to different places in London for me when I'm here, and look after my interests when I'm at sea. I'll pay you the same as I pay my chief steward plus extra when you do a delivery for me. It can be dangerous work as you have seen tonight. You won't be able to trust your best friend. Will you do it, Big John?"

'"Yes, I will, Captain. I'll be glad of the chance. You can trust me; only you and I will know I work for you. I know these docks and old London like the back of me hand. I can get through where others can't."

'The Captain rose to his feet.

'"Right, Big John, that's a deal between us. Don't ever come aboard again. Where can I find you?"

'"If you wants me in a hurry, just tell the match-seller at the end of the dock road that the Captain wants Big John."

'The Captain took a key from his pocket, unlocked a small drawer in the desk then turned to John and said, "That's for tonight's work."

'He dropped two gold sovereigns into John's hand; then, before my father could say anything, he dropped in another five.

'"Blimey, Captain! I never had so much money all at once in my whole life before. Thank you, thank you."

'"I'm sailing tomorrow night, Big John. That should keep you going until I get back in five or six weeks' time." He opened the cabin door and yelled, "Bosun, put this man ashore."

'My father walked home with his feet hardly touching the ground and his arms full of food for the family.'

Big Alf stopped writing, and once more drank deeply from his glass. Sam looked at him, the things he had read flashing through his mind, understanding slowly dawning on him.

He looked round, making sure nobody was within hearing distance, and said to his father, "Do you mean that your old man – my grandfather – was a smuggler?"

Alf looked at his son and slowly nodded his head.

"Bloody hell!" blurted out Sam. "Don't that beat all!"

They sat silent for a few minutes, and both drained their glasses. Sam got another bottle from the bar and refilled them.

As if this was a signal, Big Alf started to write again:

'"Yes, boy, my old man was a smuggler – mostly pearls and gems from Holland and the East. It was a hard life, but it paid well. He was very good at it. The Captain was always one jump ahead of those that would have liked to relieve him of his precious cargo. My father was a smuggler for over twenty-five years.'

Alf stopped writing and looked straight ahead for a good few minutes.

Eventually Sam got impatient and said, "Well, go on, then."

Alf looked quickly at his son, grunted and then started to write again:

'My old man put me to lightering when I was old enough, and that kept me busy, but, when I got to about eighteen years old, things started to puzzle me about the old man. He seemed to work funny hours. I knew he was a docker, but Mother would say, "Your father's at work," when I knew damn well no ships were being worked. He never threw his money about, but he never seemed short like most people were where we lived.

'One night I thought I would follow him. As he went out the front door, so I went out the back, and I saw him head for the dock. I followed him along the waterfront, trying to keep back and out of sight. As I passed some carts waiting for the next day's work, I suddenly realised I could no longer see him; he just seemed to have disappeared. I searched 100 yards or so further on, but there was no sign so I turned to go back home.

'As I made my way towards the carts, a big hand grabbed me by the throat and the old man's voice whispered in my ear: "What the bloody hell's your little game, Alfie boy?" he said. Without waiting for an answer, he went on: "Don't you ever follow me again, son, or I might just forget who you are and break your bloody neck. Now bugger off!"

'He threw me to the ground and was gone. I got to my feet and never stopped running until I got to the house.

'It had frightened me badly, and I did not give my father's work any more thought for nearly twelve months. Then one Saturday night I had taken our mother home from shopping and was on my way to the pub when I saw Dad pass the end of the road. When I reached the corner I stopped and watched him.

'I had just about decided that it was none of my business when I heard a voice whisper, "There he goes," and four men brushed past me and tiptoed up the road after the old man. Now I did not know what the hell to do.

'In the end I thought, "Four on to one isn't right," so I followed on behind, keeping the four men in view.

'We went up this road and down that. We seemed to be going around in circles. If those four blokes had wanted to jump the old man, they could have done so on two or three occasions; no, they were trying to find out where he was going. After twenty minutes of this cat-and-mouse game I turned the corner to see the four, now two on each side of the road, at a standstill. All was quiet. Nobody moved for a full five minutes. Then one man crossed the road to the other two; then they split up and searched up and down the road. After ten minutes of this they gave up and started to walk back the way we had come. I quickly jumped into somebody's front garden and got down behind the wall.

'As they passed me one was saying, "I just don't believe it. He can't just disappear."

'Two weeks later I came out of the pub at closing time with one of my mates and nearly knocked into the old man as he went past.

'"Hello, Dad," I yelled.

'He never flinched – just kept going.

'"Blimey! That's your old man, ain't it?" said my mate. "'E must have had a barney with your old women."

'We both laughed and walked the other way.

'A little while later I was nearing our house when I heard my sister scream: "Leave 'er alone!"

'I burst in through the front door to see one bloke holding my mother from behind while the other was slapping her about the head and face. I hit him in the back of the neck with two fists. As he went down, the other man threw Mum to one side and charged towards me snorting like a bull. I stood on the figure on the floor and sunk my boot deep into the gut of the approaching man. As his head came down towards me, I grabbed it and with all my strength buried his face in the wall. His blood flew up into my face. There was no need for any more – he was all limp.

'As I went to my mother's side I felt sick. The back door flew open and the old man stood towering in its frame. He took in the scene with a glance.

'"Right, boy," he said, "grab that one and follow me. And be quick about it."

'He lifted the one with no face, threw him over his shoulder and made for the back door. I followed with the other. Halfway down the dock road he stopped at a brick wall, opened a door and went through. I followed, and the door closed behind me. In the darkness I could just make out the old man taking something from his pocket. He lifted up a manhole cover and dropped his load into the rushing water below.

'"Down there with him, son! He'll be in the river in two minutes."

'I dropped the bloke in, turned away and was very, very sick. As I stood there heaving my heart out I felt the old man's hand on my shoulder. I was gasping for breath and the sweat was running from me.

'He said, "You'll feel better when it's all up, but don't be long, boy – there's things to be done."

'I leant against the wall, wiping my mouth, and I spluttered out, "What the bloody hell's it all about? Why should blokes want to knock Mum about?" Before he had a chance to answer, I went on: "And why the hell do blokes follow you about? And why are you working when there's no boats being worked?"

'I didn't get any further.

'"Shut your bleeding mouth, son. As I said, there's things to be done. When they're done I'll tell you. Now get ready."

'He stood on something close to the wall and cautiously looked over into the street, studying it in both directions.

'"It's all clear. Let's go."

'A moment later we were through the door and walking up the road towards the house. We saw nobody and said nothing on the short walk.

'"Are you all right, girl?" the old man enquired of Mum when we got in.

'"Yus, love, I'm not so bad. Alf just got here as they started."

'"Right, get your things together. You and the kids are leaving."

'She looked at him with an enquiring look on her face just for a brief moment, then said, "Right, John, if you say so." Then to my sister: "Come on, girl – don't stand there wiv yer mouth open. Give me a hand."

'My sister never moved, but she looked at the old man and said, "Where are we going and why? I want to stay here and—"

'Mum's hand knocked any further words from her mouth.

'"Shut your mouth, girl. If you talk to your father like that again, I'll whip yer."

'They went quickly upstairs.

'"Stand by the front-room window, son, and watch the street."

'I did as I was told without question.

'In half an hour he came to me and said, "Have you seen anything?"

'"Only a drunken sailor going down the road."

'"Right, now go out the back way and come up the road from the dock end. If you see anything, walk up on our side; if it's all clear, walk up on the other side. As soon as I see it's all OK I'll set off with Mum and the kids. We are going to the station. You keep us in sight, but don't come too close just in case those bastards turn up again."

'Once again I did as I was bid, and we got to the station and put Mum and the rest of the family on the train to her sister's in Kent without further trouble.

'Back home, the old man sat with his face in his hands. I lowered myself into a chair opposite him and waited. The candle between us gently flickering from side to side seemed to keep time with our breathing. My old man started to talk, slowly at first, then quicker, as if relieved to get it off his chest, happy to be able to tell somebody at last. The whole story was told right up to date, then he paused. When he went on again, I was a bit surprised at what he said:

'"But it's all over now, son. The Captain will be here for the last time on Saturday – morning tide. You see, boy, he's retiring and when I've made my last delivery so shall I. I have saved enough to buy a little place in the country for your mother and me. You and your sister can stay here."

'We both fell silent, thinking our thoughts.

'"Dad," I said, "How come they could never catch you? I heard one lot say, 'He just disappeared.'"

'My father chuckled to himself and replied, "Well, that's about what I did, son. You see, my brother helped to build the sewers and part of the Underground around this area of London. He showed me where the tunnels lead to and how to get in and out when I want. When somebody was getting too close, I only had to lift a cover and that was it – gone! I'll tell you what, boy: tomorrow I'll take you to a Tube station you have passed many a time but never seen."

'"Thanks, Dad. That will be bloody marvellous."

'As I lay in bed, trying to get to sleep after all the excitement of the day, I thought how great it would be to go with the old man. Little did I know that he was about to make his first and last mistake.

'The next night he took me to the station that I brought you through. He also took me down the same sewer, but we went out to the river. I remember as if it was yesterday him standing on that platform saying, "Well, boy, after Saturday I shall have no further need of this place." As he left on that Saturday afternoon he said, "Don't get any bright ideas about following me, son. You go up the pub with your mates – here, have one on me." He handed me £2. "I'll see you in the morning. Ta-ta."

'I woke on Sunday morning at about nine o'clock. Straight away I could sense something was wrong. I could usually hear and smell things going on when I woke up, but that day the house was quiet. The old man was usually first up. I got up and went downstairs. There was no sign of him anywhere. I made myself some breakfast, thinking he might be in at any time. By twelve o'clock I was getting very worried; by five I knew something bad had happened to him. I walked along the waterfront, through the docks, asking if anyone had seen him. Nobody had. Then it dawned on me that he might have gone down the Tube and somehow hurt himself and could not get out. As soon as it was dark I found my way to an air duct and made my way in.'

Big Alf stopped writing and his whole body started to shake. Sam put his arm around his father's shoulders and said quietly,

"All right, mate, take it easy. Have a rest for a bit."

He once again filled the old man's glass, pulled a packet of Woodbines from his pocket, lit one and gave it to Alf. After a few moments, dragging deeply on the fag, Alf nodded his thanks to his son, and, with great effort, he again began to write:

'As soon as I got to the end of the air duct I could tell someone other than the old man had been there. By the light of the candle, I could see some iron bars, a badly torn coat, two caps, a boot and dark, wet stains which turned out to be blood. In the little room on the platform I found my old man. They had tied him hands and feet to two water pipes and then beaten him to death with iron bars. Perhaps they had seen us going there that night when he took me to see it. Because I was with him, he may not have taken his usual care. It seems likely that they lay in wait for him, knowing that he was sure to turn up with the stuff on him. Judging by the number of iron bars, there must have been at least eight attackers.

'I fell to the ground and wept like a baby in uncontrollable fury at those that had done this thing. It took me a long time before I could bring myself to cut him down. I couldn't go to the Old Bill, knowing what he had been doing all this time, so in the end I dropped him in the sewer and he floated out into the river he loved so well. Three days later he was found washed up by Tower Bridge – a nasty accident, people said.

'"So you see, son, that's how I came to know that place was there.'

Alf laid down the pencil and drank deeply from his beer. Sam sat there pondering over what his father had written.

He lifted his glass and said, "Well, here's to Big John. Without him you could never have saved us that day, Dad."

Big Alf nodded his agreement and raised his glass.

LOVE, FATE AND MARRIAGE

"Oh, dear! Oh, dear me!" the old lady said out loud (very loud) and to herself as the very deaf will.

She sat alone in her room. It was one of those moments when life seems to be a burden that is too heavy to bear. Such moments sometimes seem to come every day when you reach the grand old age of ninety-five years.

At other times the old lady realised how well off she was, having a nice room to herself with all her own furniture and bits and pieces around her. The room was heated and had a nice sunny outlook over the garden. It was a bit draughty; but then, all places seem draughty when you're that age.

It also dawned on the old lady that she was well looked after by the rest of the family. She had more than enough to eat. She even had her breakfast in bed, and her supper drink too. The toilet and bathroom was just down the landing. She had not far to go for her needs. There was only one drag, and that was getting downstairs for her dinner each night.

Those stairs took it out of her.

During the fine days of summer she was taken out for a ride in the camper van, which had its own toilet. She enjoyed these outings.

She had no money worries, for what with her old-age pension and her blind pension she had more money than she had ever had in her life before. She had no work to do.

Looking back over the years, she felt that although on the whole life had been kind and gentle with her, it had somehow passed her by. She had been born in the backwoods of Westmorland and at a time when things were not easy, and she had moved a few miles up the road to the backwoods of Yorkshire at a very early age. Most of the hardships that working-class people had to put up with in big towns or mining villages had passed her by. There were never times when she had to go without or did not know where the next meal or pair of shoes would come from.

During the Great War five of her brothers went to France and only two came back again; then one of her other brothers moved to London in service, and she never heard from him again either.

When the old lady was twenty her mother died; and as she was the oldest girl it was left to her to look after her father and family. This was the hardest time of her life. She had a father and six brothers and sisters to cook, wash and do for. There were seven or eight shirts to wash and iron every week. Her oldest brother could never make one shirt last a week like the others, and he never gave her anything for herself. Her second brother, on the other hand, would regularly give her 2 shillings. He worked on a farm and got paid at the end of the year. Each week he would bring home vegetables from the farm.

For twelve years she did that thankless job. At first she felt it was her duty, but after two years she began to feel that she was being put on a bit. Nobody gave her a hand. She never went out, so she did not get the chance to meet boys of her own age. Therefore there was no hope of any sparking, or getting wed.

By the time the war came along she was really fed up and desperate. Her burden seemed to have no end.

After the war had been on for about twelve months or so, two of her brothers went to France to do their bit and her father died; so her burden was slightly eased.

In the last years of the war the other brothers were forced to enlist, and she found herself with just her sister to look after. This was all right for a short time, but there were two little snags to this new, easier life. The first was that she was finding it nearly impossible to make ends meet, with nothing coming in from her brothers' wages. But the second worried her much more: what would happen when the war ended and they came back again? A great fear gripped her heart when she thought about it. Although she was not one who wept easily, when night came and she got between the cold sheets of her bed and her mind dwelt on it a lump would come into her throat, her bottom lip would tremble and a salty tear would sometimes find its way down her cheek. The thought of all that cooking, washing and cleaning, and not being able to go out when she wanted, was not a pleasant one. But how was she to avoid it? That was the problem.

Her first snag, the shortage of money, she talked over with her cousin when she happened to run into her one day on the way to the Cooperative.

"Well," she said, "what you will have to do, Fanny, is to take in a lodger or two."

The old lady's face creased into a smile as she recalled this conversation of long ago. 'It's a long time since anybody called me Fanny,' she thought.

When she had a minute to herself after getting home from the shops, Fanny thought of what her cousin Mary had said. At least it would be a way of managing, although it would mean more work and cooking.

Mary had said, "You could charge 10/6 per week, and if you got women they would do their own washing and keep their rooms clean."

Fanny thought to herself, 'I will go and see Mary the next time I go into town. I must find out more about it.

Three days later, she was standing knocking on Mary's front door. At the first knock there was no reply. She knocked again – still nothing. She took a coin from her purse and tapped sharply on the glass panel. Almost at once she saw the curtain of the next-door house move. She pretended not to notice, and looked up at the bedroom windows as if willing somebody to come and answer the door.

It was beginning to dawn on her that Mary was not at home, but she thought she would give it one more try. She raised the coin, but before she could deliver the blow the neighbouring house door was flung open and a scruffy, dirty, well-built woman confronted her.

"Before yer knock the bloody door down, I'll tell yer she's out," the woman said.

Fanny was somewhat taken aback by this. She did not use bad language and did not like to hear it. She also hated people who were dirty and unkempt. What is more, she recognised this woman as a girl she went to school with.

She made no sign of recognition; instead she said politely but coldly, "Thank you. I'll come back later."

"It's no good doing that," was the quick reply. "She won't be back today. She's gone to 'er relations at Skipton for the day."

"Oh?" Fanny questioned, looking up into the woman's grimy face.

Dirty Daisy took the bait: "She's looking after 'er sister's kids while she goes to visit 'er old man in hospital. 'E got wounded, don't yer know?" she mouthed with the air of somebody in the know.

Before Fanny could respond, Daisy's face wrinkled into a sly smile of recognition and a heavy hand fell on Fanny's shoulder.

"I knows yer, don't I? You're little Fanny Haws. You went to school at the same time as me, didn't yer? I remembers you. We all called yer Little Miss Prim." She paused, folded her arms over her ample bosom, shook her head from side to side and blew through her teeth. "And that's a bloody long time ago," she continued. "Like me, you must be nearly forty, but you ain't changed a lot."

Fanny wilted under this onslaught of bad taste. She smiled weakly and thought, 'She always did make me feel small.'

"Oh, yes, you're Daisy from Station Road," she said. "Well, I suppose if Mary is not going to be in today, I'd best be on my way."

She half turned to go, but was stopped by "Was it important, then? We don't see yer round 'ere so often."

The big woman's hard green eyes fixed on Fanny until she lowered her head and looked at her hands. She was not quite sure what to say next. She could not tell lies – even white ones – and yet what business was it of Daisy's? On the other hand, Fanny thought Daisy was just the type of woman who could tell her what she had come to find out from Mary.

Fanny took the bull by the horns, swallowed her pride, coloured up a bit and, in little more than a whisper, replied, "I came to ask about lodgers."

"Lodgers!" burst out Daisy in chuckling surprise. Then she bellowed on, "Does yer want to be one, or take one in?"

She laughed so loudly that before Fanny could stop herself she said, "Do be quiet, Daisy. I don't want the whole street to know."

Seeing the look on her face, Daisy lowered her voice and said, "Sorry, lass. I didn't mean to hurt yer feelings. Come inside and I'll make us a mug of tea and we'll talk."

At first the idea of going into this person's house and having tea made Fanny shudder from head to foot, but before she had time to protest she was pulled in through the door and it closed behind her. The thing that struck her first was the smell. It gripped her by the throat until she found it difficult to breathe. It was a sour sort of smell – a cross between bad fish and rotten meat.

Daisy was saying, "'Ere, sit down there and I'll put the kettle on the fire."

She lifted a pile of papers, clothes and odds and ends from one chair, threw them on to another and dusted the seat with her dirty pinny. She then picked up the kettle from the hearth and went into the backyard to fill it from the tap.

Fanny took a quick look round the room. It reminded her of a furniture sale, like they had at the marketplace in Hellifield, only everything was covered in a thick layer of what could only be called filth.

Daisy came in, poked the fire with a big black poker and placed the kettle to the best advantage over the blazing coals.

"Now then, Fan," she questioned, "what's all this lodger carry-on, then?"

"Well," Fanny answered, "I was telling Mary that I was finding it very difficult to make ends meet nowadays, with my brothers away at the war and only my sister's money and the little that I earn at the butcher's shop three days a week. She suggested I took in a lodger or two to help out, but I have not the faintest idea of how to go about it. That's why I came to see her today."

Daisy stopped putting the tea in the pot. She stood there looking at Fanny without moving, sort of weighing up everything that she had said very carefully. When she spoke it took Fanny by complete surprise:

"How come you don't get any money from your man, then?" she enquired in a voice that seemed to be kind and somewhat out of character.

Fanny thought and said, "I never married."

There was a short silence.

Daisy said, "Fancy!" then opened her mouth to ask another question but thought better of it.

The kettle spat boiling water on to the fire, sending up clouds of steam and ash. Daisy took a holder from the oven top and lifted the kettle, still spitting, towards the teapot now standing in the hearth. She filled it.

"Damn thing!" she murmured to herself.

She put the kettle to one side, carried the pot to the table and placed a cosy over it.

"We'll just let that brew awhile." She lowered her big frame into a chair on the other side of the fire from Fanny. "Indeed you must have a job to pay your way if that's how things are with yer," she went on. "If I was you, I would do what Mary says. Now, this is what you have to do: first thing tomorrow morning, get yourself down to the post office and put a card in their window. It will only cost 1 penny a week. Put something on it like 'Lodging for a respectable young lady. Apply . . .' and put your address. Then go down to the railway and see old Bert Benson the stationmaster. You'll 'ave 'eard yer brother talk of him when he worked on the railway. You remember 'is old man used to keep the Black Horse pub when we were about sixteen years old. Well, tell him that you've got a room for a lodger or two. They are drafting women on to the railway to release men for France, poor buggers. Of course, they have some men and boys as well, but they might not suit yer so well as women, Fanny."

She got up, poured the tea and handed the cup with the saucer to Fanny, saying, "The cup's clean. I washed it special like."

Fanny sipped the hot liquid and marvelled at how good it was.

They sat and talked for about an hour or more – about the war, and about Daisy's husband and children.

At the door, when Fanny was politely thanking her for the tea and the advice, Daisy said, "I'm right sorry for you, lass. Yer were never built or brought up to take the hard knocks o' life like what I was. If there's owt I can do for yer in the future, just come and give me a knock. Bye-bye, Fanny."

She smiled and closed the door.

Fanny was quite taken aback, and those words of kindness really touched her heart. As she turned and walked down the hill, she said to herself, "Dirty, of course, she may be, but I feel I have always got a friend in Daisy.

The old lady shivered, looked out of the window, pulled her rug tighter around her legs and folded her arms. Then she let her head go back on the cushion behind her as her memory ran on.

Walking back home from Daisy's, Fanny ran through in her head what she had been told and made up her mind what she would do.

Sure enough, at five minutes to eight the next morning she was going through the post-office door with her card made out in her best handwriting clutched in her hand. Twenty minutes later found her at the railway station asking for Mr Benson. The old porter took her to Platform 1, knocked at the door and then showed her in.

Mr Benson rose from his chair and waved Fanny towards a cane-bottomed chair in front of his desk.

"Will you sit down, Mrs—?"

That was as far as he got. Fanny jumped in with "Miss – Miss Haws, Mr Benson."

"Oh, Miss Haws." There was a slight pause as he weighed her up over the top of his wire-framed spectacles. "We used to have a nice young lad working in the carriage-cleaning shed name of Haws. Would he be any relation of yours, then?"

"Yes," Fanny replied, "he's my brother."

"So! He was a nice lad. Now, what can I do for you, lass?" he questioned.

"I'm thinking of taking in a lodger or two," said Fanny, hastily adding, "women, that is. I was told that you might be able to help."

"Well, that's indeed so, Miss Haws. I have a short waiting list of men and women requiring places. Suppose you tell me what kind of accommodation you have to offer and then we can see what can be done."

He opened a drawer beside him and took out a clean plain white sheet of paper. He laid it on the blotter in front of him, reached for a pencil from the tray on the desk and looked into Fanny's eyes with an enquiring look on his face.

"I have two bedrooms that are not doing anything, with my brothers away in France. They each have two beds in them, so I could take four people really.

There's a washstand in each room and a tap in the kitchen. I'm used to cooking for up to eight or so, from when my brothers were at home."

She stopped there, not knowing quite what to say next. Mr Benson made a few notes on his paper and, with his head nodding up and down, said, "So! I see. Very good! Now tell me: would your lodgers be permitted to sit with you in the evenings, or would they be confined to their rooms after mealtimes?"

"I don't see any reason for them not to sit with my sister and me," remarked Fanny in a flat sort of tone, indicating that this thought had never before entered her head.

Neither had his next question: "What bathing arrangements would there be, Miss Haws?"

There was a slight pause. Fanny coloured up a bit and said, "We have no bathroom, but there's a tin bath that can be used in the kitchen in front of the fire. My grate has a side boiler so there's plenty of hot water."

She lowered her eyes, hoping there were going to be no more embarrassing questions like that.

"Oh, good, good," Mr Benson carried on. "Right, now let's see."

He took a small hard-backed book from the desk drawer and ran his pencil over the list. He opened his mouth to speak and was interrupted by the tinkling of the telephone on the wall at the back of the office.

He rose from his chair, waved a hand at Fanny and said, "It always happens." He lifted the receiver, pressed it to his ear and shouted into the mouthpiece: "Stationmaster here."

In the silence that followed Fanny could hear scratching noises and what must have been a voice at the other end, although it was impossible to distinguish a word of what was said. Mr Benson's head went up and down, and he murmured from time to time, "So!" . . . "Aye!" . . . "No." And then: "Aye. Well, you'll just have to put that goods train into No. 3 siding until the 9.08 has gone through, and you'll have to get another guard for the goods train." There was a slight pause and Mr Benson shuffled his feet. "What's that?" Another pause. "Well, where the bloody hell's he been, then? You just find out. I'll hang on." He shifted the receiver to the other ear, turned towards Fanny and said, "I won't keep you, lass. I've got a bit of bother with a guard on the 8.35 goods train."

Fanny just smiled and nodded.

Bert Benson looked at the ceiling, then at the floor. He tapped his fingers on the wall. After a full minute he stiffened and said, "Aye, Harry, I'm here." There was a very long gap with the stationmaster blowing through his teeth and remarking, "That's bad!" and "Bloody hell, did he?" Then: "What's his name, Harry? John Hornchurch! I remember him. Let me have a word with him, Harry. Put him on. Now then, lad, it sounds like you're in a bit of trouble. Tell me: is your sister hurt in any way? Oh, good! So! Aye, she's in at work. Aye, you did the right thing, lad." There was more shuffling of feet.

"Aye, well, I can quite see your point, but don't you worry about that. I'll get you and your sister fixed up somewhere else, if only temporarily. Just you leave your things with Harry and you get on with the job, lad. Try not to worry about it. Hand me back to Harry, will you?"

"That you, Harry? Bad business this, yer know! Something will have to be done about him. No, you leave it to me. I'll ring you back when I've fixed it up."

Mr Benson replaced the receiver in its cradle, blew a long, heavy sigh, took off his hat and wiped a hand over his forehead. He then sat down, replaced the hat and said to Fanny in a low voice, "Sorry to keep you waiting, Miss Haws."

Fanny could tell his mind was on other things. She replied, "That's all right, Mr Benson. You seem to be a very busy man."

"Aye, lass, you're right there. Now, let's see – where did we get to?" He consulted the paper in front of him and went on: "So! Oh, aye, two rooms, four beds – aye, that's it. Now let's have a look at me list."

He picked up his little black book and started to run down the list. Suddenly he stopped, looked at Fanny and spoke sharply: "How soon can you take somebody?"

Fanny jumped slightly and blurted out, "Right away, I suppose. The rooms are clean. I have only to put clean sheets on the beds and put a hot-water bottle in."

"So! Good, good," Mr Benson said, his head nodding up and down again. "Then you can possibly help me out of a spot of bother. Mind, it will mean you taking a man." Before Fanny could say anything in reply, he went on: "You see, lass, it's like this." He waved his arm at the phone. "That message I just had was about a brother and sister who work for me. They are from up Durham way, but they have been here about nine months. I got them fixed up with lodgings, but last night an old man that lodges at the same house – well, he invited himself into her bedroom

57

and tried to get into bed with her. Well, she screamed and her brother went in after him and put him in hospital. They had to leave, and now they have nowhere to stay. If you could make an exception in this case – if only temporarily – you would be helping me out a lot."

Fanny put her hands to her face in horrified astonishment and replied at once.

"Poor girl! Of course I'll take them. How old are they?" she asked.

"The girl's about seventeen and her brother's about thirty-five. He's got a bad leg – that's why he's not in the army," replied Mr Benson. "Well, that's settled, then. I'll see their things are brought round to your house this afternoon. The girl – Miss Hornchurch – will be there just after 6 p.m. Her brother will arrive at about 8 p.m. Good, good. We have been of service to each other, Miss Haws."

As he finished, the phone tinkled again. He raised himself out of the chair, lifted the receiver and shouted, "Stationmaster here. Just hold on a minute, will you?" He turned to Fanny and said, "I don't think there's anything else, Miss Haws. Just let me know if there's anything I can do for you at any time."

Fanny got up and said, "Thank you very much," and let herself out.

On the way home she felt quite excited about having someone else in the house again.

'Mind you,' she thought, 'I bet my sister Edith will not be pleased. She is funny like that.'

The first thing she did when she got home was to make up the beds and put hot-water bottles in them, for Fanny was a stickler for having things aired.

At three o'clock in the afternoon there was a knock at the front door, and Fanny opened it to be confronted by a railway porter with a handcart. He enquired if this was the residence of

Miss Haws. Fanny indicated that it was, and he said he had brought over the belongings of Mr Hornchurch, as instructed by Mr Benson. Fanny thanked him and showed him where to put them. He unloaded the cart and was soon on his way.

Fanny viewed the belongings. There were two battered suitcases (one tied with a leather strap and one with a piece of rope), one boot box tied with string, and a small hatbox.

'Not very much for two persons!' thought Fanny.

She busied herself about the house, making sure things were just right, and at 5.45 she laid the table and started to prepare the evening meal.

Just as the potatoes came to the boil, Edith came through the back door with a cheery "Hello, Fan. What's for dinner?"

"Never you mind!" replied Fanny. "Just you stay here awhile and listen to me. We have two lodgers coming to stay tonight."

Edith ignored her.

"Now, the young girl's had a bad time," Fanny continued, "so I want you to be kind to her."

Fanny went on to tell her the story as she knew it. Then Edith went to wash as dinner was almost ready.

Just before 6.30 Edith said, "There's a knock at the front door. Shall I go?"

"No, stay where you are," replied Fanny, smoothing her apron out as she went.

On the doorstep in the gloom of the evening stood a tall, well-built girl.

"Would you be Miss Haws?" she faltered in a broad Geordie voice.

"I am," said Fanny. "You must be Miss Hornchurch. Please come in."

The girl stepped in and Fanny shut the door.

"Come through into the kitchen. It's warmer there."

In the light from the two gas mantles – one on either side of the range – Fanny took stock of her first lodger. She was certainly tall – a good 5 foot 10 – and hair showing from beneath her small, round straw navy-blue hat was very fair (not blonde, but not far off). She had beautiful green eyes. Her face was very feminine with thick red lips. Her complexion was ivory white. She wore a white blouse, a long navy-blue skirt, a three-quarter-length charcoal-grey coat and a woollen shawl. Fanny thought she looked Irish, and she liked what she saw.

She waved her hand towards Edith and said, "This is my sister Edith. She's about your age. This is Miss Hornchurch, Edith."

Both girls said hello together.

"Please call me Rose," said the tall girl.

"Right," – Fanny motioned to Edith – "please take Rose up to the room next to yours and help her up with her things. Then fetch her some hot water to wash with. The meal will be ready in a very short time."

The girls clattered up the lino-covered stairs, chattering away like hens in a farmyard.

Fanny put the plates to warm, thinking about Rose. 'If her brother is only half as good-looking as she is, he will be a right charmer,' she thought.

In less than ten minutes she was dishing up the dinner. She called the girls to come to the table. They ate their first course – a nice steak pie, potatoes, green peas and thick, hot gravy – more or less in silence because both girls were hungry after a day's work; but towards the end of the rice pudding all three began to chat.

Fanny and Edith at times found it difficult to understand Rose's Geordie way of saying things, and they laughed a little at each other. So engrossed in their talk were they that when a knock came to the front door all three jumped at the sound.

Rose said, "My, how the time has gone! That must be Jonty as it's past 8.30. Can I let him in?"

Fanny nodded; she was halfway there anyway.

They heard Rose open the front door and say, "Hello, lovely lad," and a man's strong voice answered, "Hello, bonny lass. How are you? Are you sure you're all right?"

"Aye," came back Rose's excited reply, "I'm all right – really all right. How's your poor hand?"

"Oh, it's nowt, lass – just a scratch. But, now, this is grand, is it not? We have been lucky to get a place so soon," he said.

"Aye, they're ever so nice. Come through and meet them."

On hearing this, Fanny rose from her chair at the table and stood by the fireside. Rose entered the room holding her brother's hand.

"Miss Haws, this is my brother John," she said.

From the moment Fanny's eyes took him in, her heart turned over. She blushed to the roots of her hair and her knees went to jelly. Never before in all her life had a man had such an effect on her.

Gran could not help but feel a slight thrill as she recalled that first meeting. She unfolded her arms, dropped her hands into her lap and stared at them.

John was tall – 6 foot 4 – with broad shoulders and narrow hips. His hair was the same colour as Rose's and his handsome face had similar green eyes and thick lips.

'My God,' thought Fanny, 'he's a bonny man. He's like a Greek god, to be sure!'

He was dressed in the navy-blue uniform of the railway. In one hand he held his hat, and in the other was a thick leather bag with a slot along one side containing a red-and-green flag. This told Fanny that he was a guard.

He moved towards her with the rocking motion sometimes used by persons with stiff knees.

He put down the bag, and with hand outstretched said, "I'm very pleased to meet you, Miss Haws. It's very kind of you to give us a place at such short notice. We are both very grateful to you. Oh, I'm sorry – I came in the front door with my big boots on. If you just show me where the back is, it will not happen again."

Fanny took his hand and her heart somersaulted again.

"I'm very pleased to meet you, Mr Hornchurch. I am pleased that I am able to help you and your sister," she spluttered through her confusion. "Now, if you would like to put your boots and bag in the cupboard in the back kitchen, Edith will show you your room. Your dinner is ready when you are."

"Thank you very much, Miss," John said with a smile.

In just over twenty minutes he was back downstairs, washed and changed into a white shirt and grey flannels. His shirt sleeves were rolled neatly over his biceps, showing a big well-muscled arm with lots of fair hair right down to his knuckles.

The two girls by this time were getting on famously and had finished the washing-up.

"Sit here," said Fanny, pulling a chair nearer to the fire. It was the chair her father had always used. She turned to the range and lifted John's dinner from the pot of boiling water over which it was keeping hot. She placed it in front of him, saying, "There! Careful, it's very hot."

"Thank you, Miss. By gum, that smells good!"

He ate in silence with the attention of a hungry man. Fanny poured him a pint pot of freshly brewed tea with his pudding. When he had finished she refilled it with more tea and asked if he had had enough to eat.

"Indeed I have, Miss," he said with a broad smile. "I can quite honestly say I have not had a meal like that in many a long day."

Fanny smiled her pleasure and said, "Turn your chair to the fire, Mr Hornchurch."

He did so, saying, "I would like it fine if you would call me Jonty, Miss. Everybody else does."

"So it shall be, then," said Fanny.

They exchanged small talk while he finished his tea. Then he rose and said, "Well, I think I'd best go and unpack my things, and you had better do the same, Rose," he reminded his sister.

They both went up the stairs. Fanny got up and started to wash up John's plate.

"Well, Fan," remarked Edith, "I think they are both very nice. It's grand having a girl of my own age about the house instead of all men."

"Aye, you are right there. It will make a change," replied Fanny.

Edith started to giggle. She lowered her voice and whispered, "I'll tell you what: you certainly made a hit with Jonty, our Fan. He's really taken with you."

"Whatever do you mean?" came the angry response from Fanny. "You shouldn't say such silly things."

"You'll have to watch yourself, Fanny."

So saying, Edith disappeared through the back door to the outside toilet.

Fanny was a bit taken aback by what her sister had said. She had not realised that she could have had the same effect on him as he had on her. The thought thrilled her more than a little.

At ten o'clock Fanny filled hot-water bottles and took them up to the beds. Rose said she thought she would go up to bed, and Fanny made supper drinks for her and Edith. Then they retired.

Jonty sat with Fanny in front of the open fire, the heat flickering on their faces as they talked – at first about the war, then about Fanny's brothers, and finally about John's family. She asked him how he had hurt his leg, and he told her about the pit accident he was involved in when he was only fifteen years old.

In no time at all it was twelve o'clock.

"My goodness," said Fanny, "it's way past my bedtime. I must make your supper. Would you like a cheese sandwich, Jonty?"

"That would be just fine, dear lady, if it's no trouble," he replied.

As they finished their supper, Jonty told Fanny that he was not on duty until two o'clock the next day and he would not be home until two o'clock the following morning.

They went upstairs to their bedrooms after saying goodnight.

It was not until she was nearly undressed that Fanny realised that Jonty had called her Fanny when he said goodnight. As she lay in bed thinking over the day's events, she could not help but marvel at the way they had talked so easily together. Jonty had a lovely soothing voice and manner of putting his words across, and he knew when to listen. Fanny thought perhaps it was because they were of a similar age. Whatever it was, she fell asleep feeling happier than she had for a long time.

Next morning she did not see a great deal of Jonty. She was busy with some ironing when he had his breakfast. Then he went out to the Railwaymen's Club down by the football field. Fanny had told him she would have his dinner ready for him at one o'clock; he came in at 12.30, changed into his working clothes, had his dinner and was out again by 1.30. And so it went on until Saturday morning when at breakfast he told Fanny he was off for the rest of the day – in fact, he would not be on duty again until seven o'clock on Sunday evening, which would start a month of night duty.

"Well," Fanny said, "I shall be off to Settle this afternoon on the train as it is market day. I hope to get some material to make Edith a dress for her birthday, and one or two other things."

"I was thinking of doing that very thing myself," replied Jonty. "I have never been there before. I didn't know it was market day."

There was a slight hesitation, and as he opened his mouth to say something else Fanny said, "Why don't you come with me, then?"

She was surprised at herself for making the suggestion, but, before she had time to feel ashamed, Jonty came back quick as a flash: "That's mighty kind of you, Fanny. I would really like that. Perhaps I could help you carry your shopping."

They were on the station platform at 1.30 as the train came in. Jonty selected an empty carriage and helped Fanny up the steps.

At Settle they left the station, walked into the town centre and started looking around the market. Fanny could not believe it. Here she was, out shopping with a man! It was something she had never done before. Her brothers had rarely done any shopping, and they would certainly not have gone with her. When they wanted something it was "Get me a shirt, Fanny", "a pair of boots, Fanny", and "Think on! I'm not made of money." All the thanks she ever got was "What did you get that colour for?" or "You paid far too much for them" or "This shirt's too tight, lass."

Jonty seemed to be interested in all that was going on and all that Fanny was buying. He even helped her with the selection of the dress materials. When he came to buy a pair of shoes he made sure he was getting value for his money. Fanny was really impressed.

It started to rain heavily, but it was one of the few times Fanny had forgotten to bring her umbrella. In no time they were getting soaked.

"Come on, Fanny," said Jonty, getting hold of her arm and steering her through the door of a small tea shop. "Let's have some tea until it stops, or until it's time to go for the train," he insisted.

Fanny had often wanted to have afternoon tea in this little shop, but she could never afford to do so. Oh, how she enjoyed that treat – lovely hot toasted teacakes with strawberry jam, cream cakes and a pot of tea for two. It was a silver tea set, and she felt like the Queen herself.

The rain if anything got heavier, and by the time they got home, what with walking to the station at Settle and then from the station at the other end, they were wet through to their skins.

As soon as they got into the house they had to change, laughing at each other through their half-open bedroom doors. As Fanny went past Jonty's room to get another towel from the cupboard on the landing she caught a glimpse of him stripped to the waist and it had an effect on her that she had never felt before. She coloured up and her whole body trembled. She felt a strange feeling in her breasts.

And so their romance slowly developed over the next six months – nothing improper, not even kissing or cuddling, just a growing closer together and a greater awareness of each other. She liked to look at him when he wasn't aware of it; she became worried and on edge when he was late home from work.

She had seen him looking with admiring eyes at her figure. When they were talking his eyes would drop to her lips and some times to her breasts, when she would get that feeling again.

They would go to Settle together about once a month to look round the market. Often they did not buy anything at all; they just enjoyed the day together.

Just before Christmas they went again. It had been snowing most of the day, and there was a bitter strong wind blowing it into drifts. The snow was 2 to 3 feet deep in places; underfoot there was a good 6 inches.

Walking from the station into town, Fanny could see that Jonty was having some trouble walking with his stiff leg and she wanted to help him. So engrossed was she in him that she did not see that just where she was walking the road took a steep drop into a drain.

Her feet just went from under her. As she went down she felt a strong arm go round her waist, but a stabbing pain went through her left knee as it hit the road. Then she was aware that Jonty was on the snow-covered ground by her side and he was saying, "My bonny lass, are you all right? My love, are you hurt? I'm sorry, my love. I just couldn't catch you when you fell."

She looked into his green eyes, so close to her, at the concern there, and she knew at once that he loved her as much as she loved him.

She smiled up at him and said quietly, "It's all right, Jonty darling. I just bumped my knee."

She put her arms round his neck, got to her feet, and helped him to his. They stood for a brief moment locked in each other's arms.

Jonty breathed, "Are you sure, dear Fanny?" When she nodded, he went on: "We shall have to be more careful. Here, hold my arm."

She slipped her arm through his and held tight to his hand, and so they stayed during their shopping. They even sat in the train holding hands, but they did not speak for both were full of the happiness they had found in the snow that afternoon.

At the station Jonty managed to get them a lift on a wagonette to the end of their road. Fanny's knee was stiff and swollen, and she was finding it difficult to walk.

On getting to the house, they found they were alone. Jonty took Fanny's hat and coat and helped her to a chair by the fireside.

He poked up the fire and said, "We had better look at that knee, bonny lass."

He pulled a small stool from under the table and sat down opposite her with his stiff leg out in front of him. She lifted her skirt to reveal a large hole in her black stocking, and through it a very white knee of twice the normal size could be seen. Fanny drew a sharp breath at the sight of it.

Jonty said softly, "My poor darling, you have hurt it. We will have to get that swelling down. Take your stocking down, dear, while I get some water." He bathed the swollen area, gently holding her leg in his big hand.

'How gentle he is', thought Fanny, 'for such a big man!'

Just then the back door burst open and the girls came in, laughing and brushing the snow from their clothes. They stopped dead and their laughter died away when they saw Fanny.

"What's happened?" said Edith in a breathless, faltering voice.

"It's all right, lass. I just fell in the snow and hurt my knee. Jonty's bathing it to help get the swelling down. Now, just you get your coats off and start getting the tea ready," said Fanny.

That night, after the girls had gone to bed, they sat in front of the fire talking. Jonty found her hand and she gripped his with both of hers, raised it to her face, pressed it to her cheek and then, with uncontrollable want, rained kisses on that warm, gentle limb.

She felt his other hand on her head, then the warmth of his lips. She raised her eyes and looked into his face.

As the tears of joy streamed down her face, she gasped, "Oh, Jonty! Oh, Jonty darling, I do love you so."

He gathered her in his arms and their lips met in that first passionate embrace of true love.

For the next hour or so they never left each other's arms, continually kissing and confessing their love until, exhausted, they drew apart. Then Jonty made supper, after which he helped Fanny up the stairs.

Next day Fanny's knee was a lot better. The swelling had gone down nearly to normal, although it was still very sore and stiff. She was so very light-hearted and happy that it was doubtful if she would have missed the leg if it had fallen off during the night.

All that day and for weeks ahead she was a changed person, living her dream. All that she had ever dreamed of and prayed for was here and now true. She went about her work of washing, ironing, baking and cleaning as if it was something new and fresh. Whatever she was doing, she was doing it for her Jonty.

The girls were not slow to note the change in them both, and, as they were both all for it, they decided not to let on that they knew in case they somehow spoilt it for Fanny and Jonty.

As for Fanny and Jonty themselves, they said nothing of their love, and they took particular care not to say or do anything in front of the girls that could be called even slightly improper. They never touched or called each other sweet names in public; they saved those special things for when they were alone.

Their love grew stronger day by day over the coming months, through spring and into summer. They went on country walks whenever the chance presented itself. They went to magic-lantern shows and fêtes – anything where they could be together – but no dances. Jonty found dancing a bit beyond him and Fanny was not bothered anyway.

One hot Sunday in August they went for a walk over the moors and sat on the soft mossy turf. Eventually it grew so hot that they decided to return home to get out of the sun.

As they entered the house, Jonty said, laughing, "I could throw my clothes off it's so hot, my love."

"Well," said Fanny, "why not take your shirt off as the girls are not here. I love your manly chest, darling."

"I'll do that very thing, lovely girl," he said as he went up the stairs.

Fanny also went to her room to change her blouse as it was wet with sweat.

She thought, 'It's all right for him, but I can't go stripped to the waist.' Then she thought, 'But I could take off my bodice and stays. Nobody will ever know.'

And that's just what she did.

Downstairs again, Fanny made a cool lemon drink.

"My word, Fanny, that was good," said Jonty, and as she stepped over his stiff leg to hang a tea towel above the fireplace he grabbed hold of her and pulled her down on to his knee.

"Let me kiss you for it . . ." His words trailed away as he realised her body had a new softness that he had not felt before. He ran his hand up and down from her waist to her hips. "Oh, my darling, you feel marvellous."

He pulled her to him and found her lips. She wound her arms round his naked neck and shoulders. He kissed her neck, the top of her breasts and the cleavage that showed there.

Fanny felt his hand slide gently up her side until it covered her breast and began to massage it. The trembling inside her became so great that she tore herself from him and stood swaying beside the kitchen table with both hands to her face. She felt faint and the sweat was running down her face.

"My darling Fanny, I'm sorry, I'm sorry. I should not have touched you. Please forgive me."

Fanny was shaking her head. She found it difficult to speak.

"Water," she whispered.

Jonty filled a glass with water and pressed it into her trembling hands. He put his arm round her, supporting her. She drank deeply and began to feel better. She lowered herself on to the nearest chair.

"I'm sorry, my love," she murmured, "but you thrilled me so much I nearly fainted." She took his hand and pressed it to her face. "I love you so much. I need you and want you so much that I have trouble controlling myself when we are close and kissing.

He was silent for a few minutes as he stood next to her and gently stroked her hair. She could feel him trembling, and when he spoke she had difficulty hearing him.

"My darling lovely Fanny," he said, "it's the same for me. I want you so very much. My whole body hurts for you until I think it will burst. Somehow we will have to control our feelings."

He then lowered himself to the floor beside her, looked up

into her moist face and said very slowly, "Dear Fanny, please marry me."

Her eyes searched his face as if she doubted her own ears. Had the words really come from him? Were they really true?

She drew his head gently to her breast and whispered, "My Jonty, my love, I will marry you."

They stayed like that for a full ten minutes without speaking, thinking over the words spoken and the promises made.

"We will have to save some money somehow for the wedding for I have very little saved," said Fanny, and she went on: "As my father has passed on I have no one to stand for me. My oldest brother would give me away if I asked him."

In between kissing and holding each other tight they made their plans. It was decided that Fanny would write to her brothers in France before they made their engagement public. They would not tell the girls just yet, but they named a date in December that would give them time to get things sorted out.

For the next few weeks their happiness was almost complete. The only difficulty they had was trying to control their passionate feelings for each other. They were not like most young engaged couples, who saw each other two or three nights a week, and usually said goodnight at the girl's parents' door. Love had come to them both late in life; they were mature people, with no parents to tell them not to do this or that. They already lived together under one roof.

By September they were feeling the strain badly and longing for December.

One bright Saturday afternoon there was a knock at the front door. A man of smart appearance with a straight back and a well-waxed moustache presented himself. Fanny thought he looked like a soldier.

He enquired, "Miss Haws?"

"Aye, that's me," replied Fanny.

"Mrs Daisy Knight sent me, Miss. She said you might be able to fix me up with lodgings. I would be most grateful if you could find me a place. I have come down from Scotland to work on the council." He spoke in a broad Edinburgh brogue.

There was quite a long pause before Fanny answered, for she was weighing up the situation. If there was another man in the house, might it not make it difficult for her and Jonty to have so much time together? On the other hand, the extra money coming in would help them with their wedding plans – and it would only be for a couple of months. She looked at the man, noticing that he was somewhat older than she was.

"I think I can fit you in all right, Mr—?"

"Mr MacNab, Miss," he said.

"Mr MacNab, it may mean that you will have to share, unless my two girls will go in together. When would you be wanting to come, then?"

"From this coming Monday, if that's all right, and I don't mind sharing." He beamed at her.

"All right, then, Mr MacNab. I will expect you on Monday."

"Thank you very, very much, Miss," he said as if a weight had been lifted from his mind.

She watched him walk away with a definite spring in his step.

'He is happy anyway,' thought Fanny.

When the girls came home, Fanny asked them if they would like to share a room together and they jumped at the chance, having become such very good friends.

Jonty was quite pleased with the idea when he realised that he and Fanny would have more money to go towards the wedding.

It crossed Fanny's mind how nice it was of Daisy to send Mr MacNab along like that. She thought, 'When the girls go out tomorrow for their walk, I'll give them something to take to her.

Before she went to bed that night she wrote a short note to Daisy thanking her for sending Mr MacNab to her and hoping that she would enjoy the cake she was sending.

The next day, Sunday, Jonty was on early shift. Fanny got up at five o'clock, cooked him a good breakfast and made up his bait box. He had to be at the goods yard by 6.

As he kissed her goodbye, he said, "With a bit of luck I should be home again by four o'clock, darling."

Fanny busied herself about the place, cooking the Sunday dinner and helping the girls with new dresses they were making. At 1.30 they had dinner, and by two o'clock they had washed up and the girls were getting ready to go out. They left at about 3, complete with note and cake for Daisy.

Fanny liked to take a bath at times like this, when she knew she was alone and not liable to interruptions. She got down the tin bath from the nail in the yard and filled it from the boiler. Then she went upstairs, stripped off and came down with a towel wrapped round her. She put the towel over the chair, stepped into the warm water and bathed herself. She lay back, soaking, enjoying the soft warm water caressing her body.

'I wonder what my Jonty would think of my figure if he could see it now,' she thought, looking down at her full breasts, the nipples enlarged by the warm water, her flat stomach and sleek, smooth thighs.

Lying there in the warmth she began to feel very sexy, so she stood up, saying to herself, "This will never do."

She reached for the towel and started drying herself. She had just finished the last foot and had hung the towel to dry in front of the stove, when the back door opened and Jonty walked in. He was saying, "I'm home, lovely girl," but his words trailed into nothing at the sight that met his eyes. He was rooted to the spot and could not tear his eyes away from the loveliness of this beautiful naked women that stood before him – his woman, his lovely Fanny.

As for Fanny, she let out a scream.

"Jonty!" It was as if she expected him to vanish into thin air just by her uttering the word.

When he never moved, she made a grab for the towel to cover her nakedness. It had somehow become caught, so she pulled it harder and in her haste the airer was upset and everything landed on the hot stove.

"Damn thing!" cried Fanny in annoyance as she grabbed at the tea towel, two face cloths, a pair of socks and the offending bath towel before they started to scorch.

Jonty was now by her side, lending a helping hand. Her anger turned to merriment and she started to laugh. Jonty also started to laugh. In seconds they were in each other's arms, her nakedness forgotten. Fanny rained kisses on him with a fury of passion that took him aback – but not for long. He poured kisses on her naked body. Now their passion for each other had reached a point of no return; both were trembling with their need for each other. She felt his hands on her breasts, on her bottom, then between her legs. She did not care. This she did not want to stop.

She tore at his jacket, then his shirt. She felt his naked chest. He undid his belt and she pushed his trousers down over his hips. She felt his hard bottom, his flat belly, and then his hard, throbbing erection. She was on fire now. She found herself lying on the floor, pulling her lovely man on top of her. She let out a cry as he entered her, but the pain was soon over and forgotten in the delight of their first union.

When their passion was spent they lay side by side on the floor, not talking, feeling hot and breathless and both a little ashamed.

Suddenly Fanny sat up, saying quickly, "The girls, Jonty! The girls – they'll be here directly."

They got to their feet, gathered their things and were up the stairs and into their bedrooms like a shot.

While Fanny was dressing she heard Jonty go downstairs, and the next thing she could hear him emptying her bath water and putting the tub away. She went downstairs and met him at the bottom. He was carrying a jug of water with which to wash himself.

"You did not give me time to get washed before you were at me," he joked, and before Fanny could reply they heard the girls coming across the yard. Jonty whispered, "We only just made it, lovely girl," and he went on up to his room.

Jock MacNab proved to be a very nice chap. He did not have a lot to say for himself, being quite shy, but he liked to go out for a pint at night and at Sunday dinner times he and Jonty would sometimes go together. They seemed to get on very well, and he fitted in with the rest of the household. They were quite a family! Jonty and Fanny would make love whenever the chance offered itself. Their love was complete and they enjoyed its fruits.

By the third week in November Fanny had heard from her brothers in France wishing her all the best on her engagement.

"We will tell the girls and make it public at the end of the month," Jonty suggested. "We could get wed on Boxing Day."

Fanny agreed. That would stop the girls getting too worked up and yet give them time to get their own clothes together ready for the big day. Jonty also said he would ask Jock to act as best man. Fanny was pleased with the idea.

At the end of that week, when Jonty come home from his Sunday shift he found Fanny sitting by the fire. He could tell she was upset.

"Whatever is the matter, my lovely girl?" he asked softly.

At first she shook her head, but when he persisted she turned away from him and whispered, "I'm afraid I'm pregnant. I'm going to have a baby."

"Why, that's nothing to be sad about, my bonny lass. I am over the moon. It was always possible that it would happen before we were wed, my Fanny. Come now! Be glad, for it will be our baby from our true love. Anyway we will be wed in a matter of weeks. I'll ask Jock tonight and go and see the vicar on Sunday about putting up the banns. It will be our secret, my pet."

He kissed her and she felt a lot better. She had been scared about how he might take it.

'He really is a lovely man,' she thought.

They heard Jock and the girls coming across the yard, and Jonty went up to wash.

That night after their meal, Jonty managed to catch Jock in his room before he set off for his pint. When he asked him about being best man, at first Jonty thought he was going to refuse, for he just stood there looking at Jonty with a blank look on his face.

Then a smile grew from his eyes out and he said, "Well, Jonty me laddie, if you are sure that's what you'll be wanting, then I should be more than pleased to do it for ye."

He held out his hand.

Jonty took it firmly, cupped it in both of his and said, "Thank you, Jock. That's damn kind of you. I could wish for nobody better."

"I don't know so much about that," replied the Scot, and he went on: "I'll tell you one thing, man: you have got a right bonny woman there, you know. Aye, and a right good cook too!" he laughed.

Jonty let go of his hand and said, "We are not telling the girls until next weekend, so that they don't get too excited."

"You can depend on me, man. I'll no say a word until yer tells me."

On Friday Jonty did not leave for work until 10 a.m. When Fanny kissed him before parting he gave her an extra long hug and kiss, saying, "It won't be long now, bonny lass. I'll see you about midnight or thereabouts."

On Fridays Fanny liked to clean and blacklead the big grate ready for a bit of baking on Saturday morning. As Jonty had been late leaving, she had been late with the grate, and two o'clock in the afternoon found her on her hands and knees, polishing away. Her mind wandered on to what the future held, and the thought made her so very happy.

Suddenly she heard a noise behind her and she rose to her feet. A voice cried, "Fanny!"

She turned round but no one was there. A shiver ran through her. She felt scared. One hand covered her heart.

Then she laughed and said to herself, "I must have that man in my brain! I thought I heard him call me."

By eight o'clock that evening they had had their meal and were near to the end of the washing-up when Rose said, "I thought I heard a knock at the front door. Should I go and answer it?"

"Aye, will you, lass? I can't imagine who it can be at this time."

Before Rose had time to leave the kitchen they heard the front door open and Jock's voice saying, "Hello there. Who was it you'll be wanting?" And then: "Aye, right." He came into the kitchen and said, "Miss Haws, there's a man at the door to see you – a Mr Benson."

"My word!" Fanny remarked, taking off her pinny. "Whatever can he want?"

"Good evening, Mr Benson," she said at the door. "What can I do for you?"

"Good evening, Miss," spluttered the stationmaster. His errand was not a pleasant one and he was having difficulty in knowing where to start. "It's rather a delicate matter, I'm afraid, Miss."

He was about to go on, but Fanny interrupted him: "Perhaps

you would like to step into the front parlour for a few minutes?"

"Aye, that would be best, Miss. We will not be overheard there."

Fanny put a match to the gaslight, shut the door and motioned Mr Benson to a chair.

"No thanks, Lass," he said in a low voice, and Fanny wondered at the troubled look on his face.

"I take it Miss Hornchurch is at home, for this concerns her most of all."

Fanny nodded, and a strange fear began to form in her mind. One hand went to her heart, the other to her throat.

He went on: "I thought it best to tell you first, Miss. As she is only a young lass and he her brother, I though it might be better coming from you."

Fanny lowered herself into a chair as her legs turned to water. Her eyes were wide and slightly glassy.

She heard her own voice whisper from far, far away, "Whatever has happened?"

There was a pause and Mr Benson half turned from her, his chin on his chest, both hands in front of him clutching his cap. When he spoke, his words came slowly and softly.

"I'm afraid, Miss, there's been an accident on the rail at Crewe. Mr Hornchurch has been killed."

For a split second his words did not register, then a vice-like hand gripped and crushed her heart.

She murmured, "Jonty," as her throat closed, the room swam and the floor came up to meet her as she fell head first into blackness.

Gran removed the shawl from around her, moved to the window, pushed it wide and stood there gasping for breath as the tears ran down her face.

"Silly old fool!" she sobbed. "It always upsets me when

my memories go back to that day, and yet I can't stop myself."

To say that Mr Benson was shocked at the way things were turning out is putting it mildly. He thought he had worked it all out for the best: tell Miss Haws, she would tell the girl, and that would save him getting too much involved. But things were not going to plan, for here he was with a motionless women lying at his feet. But then, of course, he did not know about Jonty and Fanny.

Blind panic was the first thing that hit him. He wanted to scream for help, then get off up the road as fast as his legs could carry him. As he opened the door he more or less fell over Jock, who was just going off for his pint.

"She's fainted," he blurted out.

Jock entered the room and knelt beside Fanny's crumpled figure.

"What the devil have you been saying to her, man?" he said angrily as he gathered her up in his arms and placed her gently on the sofa.

Mr Benson replied, "I came to tell her that Mr Hornchurch had been killed in an accident."

"My God! No wonder the poor wee lass passed out." He went to the door and called out in a sharp commanding voice, "Edith, come through here quickly, lass."

She appeared at the parlour door in an instant.

She opened her mouth to speak, but Jock cut her short with an upraised hand and said, "Your sister's fainted, lass. Just take care of her. Loosen her clothes and rub her hands. She will soon come round."

He led Mr Benson by the elbow out into the hall.

"Do you know that Jonty's sister lives here?" he asked.

"Oh, aye – you see, it was really her I came to see. But I thought it would be better coming from Miss Haws, you see. I didn't reckon on this happening."

"Come into the kitchen and I will tell her," said Jock.

They went through to the kitchen just as she was coming in from the backyard.

"Oh, hello, Mr Benson," she said in her usual bright voice.

Jock took her arm and motioned her to a chair. He took both her hands and in a soft, gentle whisper said, "Now it's time for you to be very brave, bonny lass."

Mr Benson wondered how such a big man could be so gentle and calm.

Jock went on: "There's been an accident on the rail."

Rose began to tremble. She shouted quickly, "Jonty! Jonty – is he hurt?"

Her eyes were looking deep into his, searching, and she knew the answer before he said, "I'm afraid it's worse than that, lass. Your brother has been killed."

Rose threw herself at him, beating his chest and screaming.

"No! No! It's not right. It can't be – not our Jonty."

The tears were cascading down her face. Jock put his arms round her and drew her to him. After a few seconds she stopped fighting and just sobbed deeply.

Edith came running in.

"Jock, Jock, I can't rouse her," she shouted. Then: "What's wrong?" she asked, seeing Rose crying.

Jock ignored her and said to Mr Benson, "Go off for the Doctor right away."

Mr Benson turned and hurried from the room out of the front door and down the road, glad to be free of the house where his message had brought so much havoc, glad to be doing something that he had not had to work out for himself. He was a good stationmaster, but away from the railway he was like a fish out of water.

Jock gently lowered Rose back into the chair, talking kindly to her all the time. In a while he drew Edith out of the kitchen and into the hall, where he told her of the accident.

She was very shocked and wept as much for her sister as for herself, knowing what she and Jonty meant to each other.

Jock and Edith both went into the parlour and tried again to rouse Fanny. She looked near to death as she lay there not moving and very white. Jock sent Edith off for a blanket and a hot-water bottle. He explained to her that she would have to go with Rose to Crewe to formally identify the body as it would not be very nice or fitting for her to go on her own. Edith then went and sat with Rose while Jock stayed with Fanny.

In fifteen minutes the Doctor arrived with the stationmaster. He was quickly on his knees beside Fanny, feeling her pulse and listening to the beat of her heart. He tried smelling salts and moved her this way and that, but to no avail.

"We will have to get her to bed," he said.

After this was done, Mr Benson managed to get Jock on his own.

"Will it be all right if I leave you to it now, lad?" he asked. "I'm that sorry about what's happened. Aye, it's a bad job. So! Aye! I'll send trap round for the two girls in the morning in time for the 9.10 train. It will cost them nowt, yer knows. How will you manage tomorrow? Miss Haws is not fit to be left, I shouldn't think. Aye! I'll tell you what, lad: she has a friend called Daisy and I'm sure she would see to her while you're at work and the girls are away. If you agree, I could call on my way home just now."

"Aye," replied Jock. "I know Daisy. It was through her I got my place here. I would be very glad if you would call on her, Mr Benson."

"Right, lad, I'm away, then. Please, God, things will soon improve. I don't know what we would have done without you, Jock."

So saying, he left by the front door into the night.

The Doctor stayed with Fanny for more than half an hour, trying first one test and then another. Then he announced that he would have to get his partner to come and have a look at her.

"She seems to be in severe shock," he said. "Don't leave her, and if she comes round, don't move her or upset her in any way. Above all, keep her warm. I'll be back within the hour."

He packed his little black bag and left.

Edith stayed upstairs with her sister, and Jock stayed with Rose, who was now regaining control of herself. Jock put the kettle on the stove and made a cup of well-sugared tea for each of the girls and himself. He sat down beside Rose and drank his, wishing all the time it was a wee dram.

He had just taken the cups back to the scullery when there was a knock at the front door. He hurried through, thinking it was the Doctor returned, but instead he found Daisy standing grim-faced on the step.

"I came as soon as I could after Mr Benson called, Jock," she boomed in her coarse voice. "What the hell's been going on here, then, my lad?" she continued.

"Come on in, Daisy lass. It's good of you to come so quick," said Jock, holding her arm and guiding her into the dim hallway.

She stood motionless and quiet, just nodding her head from time to time and drawing in quick breaths through her teeth as Jock related the tragic events of the evening.

When he had finished, she looked at him somewhat puzzled and said bluntly, "It's a bloody shame right enough, Jock, and I could not be more sorry for the poor lad and his sister." She paused, looking him straight in the eye, and then went on: "But I can't for the life of me see why it should affect Fanny so."

Jock looked at her and shrugged his shoulders. Then, plunging his hands deep into his pants pockets, he turned away from her and said, "Well, Daisy, there's a bloody good reason why."

"Come on, then – what is it? Out with it, man."

He turned back to her and said, "They were very much in love, Daisy, and they had asked me to be best man at their wedding. The banns were going up this weekend."

"Well, I'll be—! Of course! That's got to be it!" Daisy exclaimed, blowing through her teeth. "That's why the poor lass has taken it so badly – she's heartbroken." So saying she walked past him to the kitchen. "Don't you worry yourself, Jock. I'll look after her from now on, until she's all right."

"Aye, I know you will. You're a damn good sort, Daisy. Thank you," replied Jock.

He felt in his pocket for his pipe. As he filled it, he felt a lot more relaxed for having Daisy in the house.

A short while later the two doctors came, and Daisy took them up to see Fanny. They were there a good hour or more, carrying out tests and whatnot.

When Daisy came back into the kitchen her jaw was set, and her narrowed eyes had an angry glint in them.

"It's my belief them two don't know what the bloody hell they're up to," she hissed at Jock so that the girls couldn't hear.

"Is Fanny going to be all right?" asked Rose quietly.

"Don't you fret about that, lass. She's certainly going to be right enough. It's just that some people can't cope with shock like others. By this time tomorrow she'll be up and about." In her heart she knew differently, but she went on, scarcely drawing breath: "Now, you girls had best have a drink and get to bed. You have a big day in front of you tomorrow." The commanding note in her voice left them in no doubt as to what they should be doing next.

Jock sat with Fanny until midnight while Daisy had a rest, then she took over for the rest of the night. Fanny just lay there with no movement at all, breathing deeply as if sleeping, but Daisy knew she was in a coma. When morning came she woke the girls in plenty of time to get the train. Breakfast was ready for them when they came down.

Jock had not gone long when the trap turned up to take the girls to the station. When Daisy had seen them on their way, she took some warm water up to Fanny and gently sponged her face and hands. All the time she talked to her as if she was conscious. After doing all she could to make her comfortable, she made herself a mug of tea and some toast. She cleaned out the grate and made up the fire, and she started thinking about dinner for when Jock came home at midday.

There was a knock at the front door and the Doctor let himself in.

"Morning, Daisy," he said. "Has there been any change?"

On the other side of the bed, Daisy folded her arms over her chest, looked him straight in the eye and said, "No, and you don't expect there to be when she's in a coma, do you?"

The Doctor looked at her sharply. He was not sure that he liked her tone of voice. "You don't miss much, do you, Daisy?" he said. "Yes, it's right enough: she is in a deep coma, but why she should be, and how I'm going to get her out of it, at the moment I have no idea."

"I know why she's like that," bellowed Daisy. "She's heartbroken. They were to be wed, don't you see?"

"Oh! Oh! So that's it, then. Now, that explains a lot – it certainly does." A little smile crept over his face.

"I don't know what you've got to smile about," snapped Daisy, her eyes flashing.

"Well, there's something even you don't know about, Daisy: she's going to be a mum."

"Well, I never!" burst out the large woman. "If that don't beat all! I should never have guessed it. The point is, how are we going to get her out of it?" She went on, looking now at Fanny's motionless form lying there: "They do say that another shock will sometimes do it."

"That's right, Daisy. Have you any ideas?"

Daisy said nothing, but the Doctor could see her mind working.

She muttered more or less to herself, "No, I can't bring anything to mind. There was the time when . . . No, that's no good." She pondered some more, then slowly her face started to brighten. "When we were at school together I used to tease her rotten, and there was one thing that used to frighten her to death. . . ."

After she had explained her idea to the Doctor he shook his head doubtfully and said, "I don't know about that, Daisy. It sounds a bit drastic. There's no telling what might happen with a shock like that. Why, she might even lose the baby. No, I think we had best forget that until I find out more about it, but if she doesn't come round soon we must find a way of feeding her."

"Well, there's naught else I can bring to mind as yet," Daisy replied with a sigh.

The Doctor came twice a day and gave her an injection to feed her. Edith helped to look after Fanny, taking it in turns with Jock and Daisy to sit with her.

Rose did not come back after Jonty's funeral. She went to stay with an aunt.

They tried all sorts of ways to bring Fanny round, but there was not even the slightest reaction from her.

One day, after Edith and Jock had left for work, Daisy washed and sponged her all over. When she had dried her she looked down at the poor, helpless, limp figure, and a lump came to her throat. She could not remember the last time she wept, but she was near to it now.

She said in a whisper, "Ee, lass, it really grieves me to see you so."

She swallowed hard and covered Fanny up again. She picked up the bowl of water and the towel and started towards the door, where she stopped and looked back at Fanny. She slowly turned and set down the bowl. She started to pace back and forth in front of the bed. She had made up her mind, but how was she to start? She had to be quick because the Doctor would soon be arriving. She looked at Fanny again. Then she continued to pace up and down, wringing her hands together.

Then in a flash she was beside the bed. She threw back the bedclothes, grabbed hold of the limp body by the shoulders dragged it to a sitting position and started to shake it like the devil had possessed her.

Her face was close to the lolling head of Fanny and she was shouting at the top of her voice: "Keep out of my way, bloody Miss Prim, or I'll have your drawers down and show your arse to the boys." At the second attempt, Daisy felt a slight stiffening of Fanny's body. She shouted even louder. The head stopped wobbling about and the lips began to move. Daisy was about to shout again when Fanny's eyes opened.

For a split second she looked at Daisy and then started to scream at the top of her voice: "No, no, you horrible girl! Get away from me!"

She started to struggle.

Daisy threw her strong arms quickly round her and, drawing her to her bosom, soothingly said, "It's all right, lovely girl, it's all right."

Slowly Fanny calmed down, and they clung to each other with tears flooding from their eyes – and that's how the Doctor found them when he came through the door.

He could scarcely believe his eyes. He stood there open-mouthed, and then with a catch in his voice he said, "Daisy, Daisy, it's a pure miracle. I can't believe it."

"Not quite a miracle, Doctor," sobbed Daisy, desperately trying to control herself, "just something from the past. You had best check her over while I go and get her some tea and toast." So saying, she laid Fanny back on the pillow, smiled at her and patted her hand. "I'll not be long, lass," she added.

She got up and made for the door, wiping her tear-stained face on her dirty overall.

Edith and Jock were both overjoyed at the good news that greeted them on their return from work. They wanted to rush upstairs to Fanny, but Daisy had to warn them, on doctor's orders, to be very, very careful, for the least upset or excitement might send Fanny back into a coma.

For the next few days Fanny said very little to anyone, and Daisy quite often found her crying, but she never let on that she had noticed anything. They were all very gentle with her. By Saturday she was able to sit in a chair by her bed, but she looked a pitiful figure. Gone was Miss Prim. Her formerly straight back was bent; her once proud head was no longer held high, but slumped on to her chest looking only at the twisted hands in her lap.

After a fortnight she was doing her housework and cooking again, and Daisy only called in on one or two days each week.

One Saturday morning at about nine o'clock Daisy opened her front door to go to the shops, and who should be coming up the road driving a smoking steamroller but Jock! They waved to each other and shouted hello above the noise of the hissing monster. Jock motioned to Daisy to wait, brought the roller to a stop and climbed down.

"I'm glad I've seen you, Daisy," he said, wiping his hands on a cotton rag. "I'm a mite worried about Fanny. She's not at all right – no way. She's not the same lass at all. She never goes out and I'm damned sure she eats nowt. Sometimes when Edith and I come home at night she's sat in the dark in the same chair as she was in when we went to work. She has never moved all day, I'm sure of it, and, Daisy, I wake up in the night and hear her sobbing her heart out. It really breaks me up to hear her. I think a lot of Fanny and I wish I could do something to help her."

The concern in his voice touched Daisy; she looked at him in a different light.

"Aye, you're right, Jock. I've seen it too. Her spirit is completely broken, don't you see. I fear for her. We will have to find a way to help her, man – but how?" A thought then came into her head, and she said, "Did you know she is expecting, Jock?"

"Nay, nay, that I didn't!" he exclaimed, more than somewhat taken aback.

"Well, say nowt to no one, but it might have something to do with her being like this."

"I'll no say a word. Poor wee lass! She must be worried stiff. If there's anything I can do, Daisy, just you tell me."

"Don't worry, Jock – I'll do just that," she replied, and she carried on down the road.

On Monday Daisy made a point of calling at Fanny's house at about three o'clock in the afternoon. She knocked on the front door twice very loudly, but there was no response.

'She surely can't be out!' thought the big woman.

She went round into the yard and knocked at the back door. Still no answer! She tried the door handle and the door opened.

She pushed it wide and called, "Fanny, Fanny, are you there, love?"

There was no answer, but Daisy thought she heard a noise. She went into the kitchen, and there was Fanny, sitting on one of the old wooden chairs in front of the fire, which either had gone out or had never been lit that morning. Breakfast dishes were still where they had been left, which might have been the norm for Daisy's house but was unheard of in Fanny's. She sat there with her head hung down, her hands twisted round a handkerchief in her lap. Her clothes were not fastened properly; her stockings were all wrinkled; her hair was long about her shoulders.

Daisy whispered, "Fanny, are you all right?"

She never moved.

"Fanny, what are you doing?" Daisy bellowed.

She touched Fanny's arm and at this Fanny jumped as if suddenly wakened from a deep sleep.

"Oh, who's that?" she whispered in a voice so weak that Daisy could only just make out what she said. "What are you doing here so early, Daisy?"

"It's not so early, lass. It's getting on for 3.30 in the afternoon and it is bloody near time you shook yourself and did your hair. You're looking like a damn tramp."

As soon as the words were said she felt sorry, for Fanny was like a child that had been scolded for something she did not understand. The blank look in her tear-filled eyes made Daisy's heart turn over. She put her big strong arms round Fanny's shoulders as Fanny buried her face in Daisy's coat and sobbed uncontrollably.

"There, there, Fanny! Don't take on so, lass. You've had a bad knock, but you've got to try and live with it. Think of your baby. You have got to keep yourself fit for the babe."

Fanny was shaking her head, and through her sobbing she breathed, "I don't want it, I don't want it!"

Daisy pushed her away, took her face wet with tears in her hand and lifted her chin. She looked her straight in the eye and said in a voice that sounded somewhere between a growl and a snarl, "Don't you ever let me hear you say anything like that again! I know you're not wed, but that babe came from true pure love between Jonty and you. It's Jonty's baby, and it's all you have got of him now." She lowered her hands, placed them gently on Fanny's stomach and went on: "You have got to love that babe, Fanny, for two people now."

Fanny covered Daisy's hands with hers, sniffed and said in a sad little voice, "I want to, Daisy, but it's not going to have a father. What will people say? I will have to go away where nobody knows me, but I don't have much money. Jonty and I were saving up for the wedding, but there's not enough to take me far or keep me while I have my baby. Oh, why did he have to be taken from us like that?"

"Aye, fate has given you a bad knock and no mistake."

Daisy paused for a full two minutes or more, looking into Fanny's face as she fought to control her tears. Then she went on, talking slowly and deliberately so that Fanny had no chance of misunderstanding what she was saying.

"They say, Fanny, when one door closes another opens up. What you have got to do is get wed – and quick." She held up her hand as Fanny looked at her in horror and started to protest. "Just shut up and listen. I know you think you can never love anybody else, and you're right, lass – you'll never ever find a love like the one you have lost – but I'm talking about getting wed. It so happens that your other lodger, Jock, thinks the world of you – although you probably never knew it. Now, if he was to ask you to get wed, all your troubles would be over. Aye, you can take it from me that he is a kind and gentle man. Just you think on it, lass, while I help you with your hair."

"I couldn't do it, Daisy – I just couldn't to it."

"Your baby would have a father – and he was going to be your best man, you know. You would be looked after, and there would be nobody the wiser. Think on it, Fanny. Think on it."

Together they washed up, lit the fire and started to get the meal ready.

At last Daisy said, "I'll have to go, lass. I've a family to look after, don't you know? I'll call in and see you in the morning. Aye, think on what I've said and don't worry about him asking you. He will."

Fanny thought on it all right – she couldn't think of anything else – and when Jock came home she looked at him with new interest. Daisy was right: he was a kind and gentle man. He was hard-working, clean and smart in his dress.

'I suppose I could do a whole lot worse,' thought Fanny.

Next morning, as Jock turned the corner of the street on the way to the council yard to start work, he was more than a little taken aback to see Daisy waiting a little way along the pavement.

"Morning, Jock," she said cheerfully. Without waiting for a reply she went on: "You and I have got to talk; so if it's all the same to you, I'll walk to the yard with you."

"Aye, all right, Daisy. Thank you for going to see Fanny yesterday. She seems a lot brighter this morning."

"Well, that's what I want to see you about, Jock," Daisy bellowed against the strong winter wind. "Fanny's not going to stay like that for long unless you do something about it." Before he had a chance to get a word in, she waved her hand and carried on: "That poor lass is in a bloody bad fix: she's going to have a baby in about seven months from now and she's not got a husband. Nobody but you, me and the Doctor knows she was even planning to wed. What are people going to say? She feels she'll have to go away, but she's not enough brass to do it, and where's she going to go?" Jock opened his mouth, but Daisy went on: "She doesn't want the babe, and quite frankly, lad, I'm scared of what she might try and do." She stopped and turned to face him and said, "I'm dead scared, lad."

"Nay, nay, Daisy, you don't mean she'd try and get rid of the bairn, or try and kill herself!"

"That's just it, Jock," Daisy replied.

"What can I do, Daisy? What can I do?"

"Well, there's a very simple answer to that, my lad, which would solve all her problems – and it would solve yours too."

"Mine, Daisy? I don't understand," said Jock, puzzled.

"You're a shy man, Jock. That's why you've never wed. I'm sure you would like a place and a woman of your own."

He stopped walking and turned to the big woman as the meaning of her words began to sink in.

He spoke in a whisper as if talking to himself: "You mean I should wed Fanny? I admit I think a whole lot of her, but I could never take Jonty's place. I'd be good to her and all that, and there's no denying that I'd like a wife and have done for many a year, but I never had enough guts to go courting a lass. No, Daisy, she'd never think about it."

"You're wrong, lad, you're wrong. Don't you see, she has no hope at all at the moment? You're her last chance. You ask her, Jock, and, if you want a good wife, housekeeper and cook, then persuade her, Jock – persuade her. She's a good woman like you are a good man."

He stood there scratching his chin, and then: "All right, Daisy, I'll do it tonight. I'll damn well ask her."

"Good man!" said Daisy, and she slapped his arm as she turned to go.

"Thank you, Daisy. You're a right good lass," he called after her.

After work, on returning to the house, Jock was surprised to find the table laid, the fire blazing away and things tidied up like they used to be.

Fanny greeted him with "Hello, Jock. You're a bit early. Dinner's almost ready. Get yourself washed while I dish up."

"Oh, right, Fanny," stammered the Scot.

He noted that there was a change in her. There was no smile, her eyes were still red with dark rings round them, but her hair was more tidy, her back more straight and her mouth was set in a determined line. He guessed that she had made up her mind about something, and the thought frightened him a bit. He prayed that she had not made up her mind to do something silly.

As he climbed the stairs he said to himself, 'You've got to ask her tonight, man. It's got to be tonight – before she has time to do something daft.'

During dinner Edith tried to talk to Fanny, but there was little response. She and Jock managed a few words, but the conversation soon petered out and the meal was eaten in silence. It gave Jock time to think over what he was going to say to Fanny when the time was right. He was quite pleased when Edith asked Fanny if it would be all right to go along to see her friend who lived two or three streets away.

Fanny nodded her agreement and said, "Don't be late back, mind."

Edith said she would not, and in quarter of an hour she was gone.

Jock thought to himself, 'Now's your chance, man.' The very thought made him tremble. His hands became wet and the sweat stood out on his forehead.

Fanny sat in the chair by the side of the grate, her face was almost expressionless and her eyes gazed into the fire. Jock was still sitting at the table, pretending to be reading the paper he had bought at a shop near the council yard. He was desperately trying to pull himself together, trying to summon up the words and the courage to say them. He just did not know where to start. It was all so new to him. He had never courted a lass – not even walked out with one before. He wished he was going to the pub for a pint or a wee tot of the hard stuff.

Fanny reached out for the big poker resting in the grate. She stirred the fire and poked out the ash; then she lifted the lid of the coal box. It was empty.

"There!" she said. "I thought I would forget to fill you before it got dark."

She rose to her feet and lifted the heavy wooden box. Jock was beside her in a flash.

"I'll see to that, Fanny," he burst out, with a tone of command in his voice that surprised himself as well as Fanny.

"Thank you, Jock," she replied quietly.

He filled the box from the coal-hole in the yard and returned it to the hearth.

As he put it down and lifted the lid he looked at Fanny and with genuine concern said, "You shouldn't be lifting heavy coal boxes like that in your condition, Fanny."

Fanny dropped the shovel she had just picked up, rose abruptly to her feet, and with eyes blazing said, "Who told you that?"

Jock remembered that he was not supposed to know, and he coloured up to the roots of his hair.

Before he could answer her, Fanny went on, her voice rising high – too high: "I guess it was that Daisy."

She turned her back on him as the tears started to well in her eyes.

"I'll tell her a thing or two. It's high time she learnt to mind her own business instead of poking into other . . ." Her voice trailed off as she fought to remove the handkerchief from her sleeve.

Jock stood behind her as her shoulders heaved up and down.

"Nay, nay, lass, please don't fret yourself. Daisy has been very good to you, and it was only because she was trying to help you that she told me." Fanny nodded as he went on: "You see, I went to see her because I was that worried about you. That's when she told me." He paused, licking the sweat from his top lip. He rocked from one foot to the other, his hands rubbing up and down his thighs. "You see, Fanny, I'm very fond of you and I was wondering if it might not be a good idea if we was to get wed."

He stood there looking at her back. She never moved, but she had stopped crying and was just sniffing.

Jock hurried on: "I know I can never be to you what Jonty was, but I'll be kind to you always and look after you with all my health and strength. And when the baby comes, nobody will know it's not mine. I don't expect you to love me, Fanny, or even – well, you know, sleep with me, like. It's just that I want a wife and you need a husband, that's all."

He shrugged his shoulders. His words had dried up. He looked at her back for a few minutes, then turned slowly to the grate and proceeded to stoke the fire. He stayed there on one knee, watching the black smoke disappearing up the huge flu, wondering if he had said enough or too much.

So they stayed for a full five minutes, neither moving, both wrestling with their own thoughts. Then Fanny slowly turned and moved towards his crouched figure. She put her hand on his shoulder, and not until then did he realise she had moved.

He started and looked up at her tear-stained face. She was looking past him into the fire.

Her voice was soft and trembling as she whispered, "I will never love you, Jock, or anyone else, but you are a good man and, if you are sure you realise what you are doing, I'll wed you for the sake of Jonty's baby. If when the baby is born, or at any time in the future, you wish to go, just be up and go. I will not stop you or try to follow you. When we are wed I promise you I will be a good wife to you as long as you want me, and never more will we speak of what has passed. Thank you, dear Jock."

She turned on her heel and left the room.

Within the month the banns were read and they were married. There was gossip circulating about how quick it was, and didn't they keep it quiet? and fancy her marrying her lodger! but after a week or two it was all forgotten among the miseries of the war.

Fanny very gradually became her old self, and each baking

day she would send something round to Daisy and her family, no matter how small.

Jock proved to be a good husband in many ways. He made no demands upon Fanny. She was having attacks of sickness and high blood pressure, but as the seventh month approached the Doctor began to feel more easy. Then, during a severe thunderstorm in late June, she had a premature birth. The baby was born dead. Everybody was dismayed, but to Fanny it was another great blow. She had been so looking forward to mothering Jonty's baby, but now she had nothing of Jonty apart from her memories. It was almost as if he had never existed. If it had not been for her sense of duty to Jock, her husband, she would have ended it all there and then.

For nearly forty years they lived as man and wife. They eventually had a baby son. Jock was a good provider to her, and she was a good wife to him. Neither had any complaints, but so many times Fanny would daydream of what might have been if fate had not dealt her such a tragic blow.

Gran turned from the window and felt her way round the bed.

"Oh – oh, dear me!" she sighed.

She lay down and pulled her shawl over her.

"Well, I'm just waiting for one thing now," she said out loud, "and then I'll see him again."

Her head rested back on the pillows behind her, her jaw dropped open and she slept.

Two weeks later she passed away in her sleep, with a lovely smile on her face.